D1138344

grk
and the
Pelotti gang

Other titles by Josh Lacey

grk

and the
Pelotti gang

Josh Lacey

Andersen Press · London

First published in 2006 by
Andersen Press Limited,
20 Vauxhall Bridge Road, London SWIV 2SA
www.andersenpress.co.uk

This edition published in 2013

All rights reserved. No part of this publication may be reproduced,
stored in a retrieval system, or transmitted in any form or by any
means, electronic, mechanical, photocopying, recording or
otherwise, without the written permission of the publisher.

Copyright © Josh Lacey, 2006

The right of Josh Lacey to be identified as the author of this
work has been asserted by him in accordance with the
Copyright, Designs and Patents Act, 1988

British Library Cataloguing in Publication Data available

ISBN 978 184939 736 0

Mixed Sources
Product group from well-managed
forests and other controlled sources
www.fsc.org Cert no. TT-COC-002227
© 1996 Forest Stewardship Council
FSC

Typeset by FiSH Books, Enfield, Middx.
Printed in the UK by CPI Group (UK) Ltd, Croydon, CR0 4YY

Chapter 1

The Banco do Brasil had three guards.

The three guards wore blue uniforms with silver buttons. Each of them carried a pair of handcuffs, two tear gas canisters and a pistol.

It was a hot afternoon. Inside the bank, the air conditioning was turned up to full, but the air was still steamy. Most of the clerks had big patches of sweat on their shirts. The customers fanned their faces with their hands.

The three guards were tired. They stared at the pretty girls who came into the bank. They chatted to the customers, discussing the weather or the news or last weekend's football results. They dreamed about dinner. It was an effort just to keep their eyes open.

When a voice shouted, 'NOBODY MOVE!' the three guards didn't know what to do. They looked around, trying to see who was shouting at them. The voice shouted again, even louder, 'I SAID, NOBODY MOVE! STAY EXACTLY WHERE YOU ARE!'

One of the guards reached for his gun. Immediately, a bullet flew through the air and smashed into the wall behind him, knocking out chunks of brick and plaster. The voice shouted again, 'DIDN'T I TELL YOU NOT TO MOVE?'

'I'm sorry,' whispered the guard.

'No moving,' said the voice. 'And no talking. Do you understand?'

The guard wanted to say 'yes' but he knew that he wasn't supposed to talk. So he nodded.

'Good,' said the voice. 'I want everyone to lie on the floor. Down on the floor! Right now!'

They did what they were told. The guards and the customers and the clerks and the manager – they all lay down on the floor. Only three people were left standing. Three men. They wore black suits and white shirts and black ties. They had black masks covering their faces. They were holding Uzis. (An Uzi, in case you don't already know, is a small and very effective machine-gun, capable of firing six hundred rounds per minute.)

One of the masked men pointed his Uzi at the three guards. He said, 'You move, I shoot. You talk, I shoot. Understand?'

The three guards nodded.

Another of the masked men strolled over to the bank manager and said, 'Open the safe. Now. Understand?'

'Ye-ye-ye-yes,' stammered the manager. Ever since he was promoted to manager of the Banco do Brasil, he had been expecting a robbery, but that didn't make it any less terrifying. 'Of-of-of cour-cour-course I understa-sta-stand.'

'Don't talk,' said the man in the black mask. 'Just open the safe.'

The manager nodded. 'Thi-thi-this way.'

Together, the manager and the man in the black mask walked to the back of the bank. They went to the vault where the money was stored. There, the man in the black mask filled five big brown sacks with cash. One by one, he carried the five full sacks back into the bank.

The first robber picked up two sacks. The second robber picked up two more and said, 'Let's go.' They ran towards the door.

The third robber picked up the fifth sack. He had only one arm, so he could only carry one sack. Where his left arm should have been, he had an empty sleeve. Carrying his sack of money, he ran after the others. When he reached the door, he stopped and put the sack on the ground. He looked up at the CCTV camera that recorded everyone who walked into the bank.

He pulled off his mask and threw it on the floor.

He stared into the lens of the camera.

He smiled as if he was posing for a photograph.

Every policeman or policewoman in Brazil would recognise his face. They would recognise his lean cheeks and his black hair and his bushy eyebrows. Most of all, they would recognise the crazy look in his eyes. They would say, 'Oh, no.' They would say, 'Not him.' They would say, 'Pelottinho is back in Brazil.'

Pelottinho.

That name would be enough to send shivers through the spine of any policeman or policewoman in Brazil.

His real name was Felipe Pelotti, but everyone called him Pelottinho. 'Pelottinho' means 'little Pelotti'. Pelottinho was the youngest and craziest of the three Pelotti brothers, the most successful gang of bank robbers in Brazilian history.

Pelottinho lifted his Uzi and fired a stream of bullets

directly into the CCTV camera.

The lens exploded. Glass splattered everywhere. The camera drooped and swung in the air, attached to the wall by just a couple of bright green wires.

Pelottinho laughed. His laughter was loud and carefree and quite insane. Tucking his gun into his belt, he grabbed the sack of money and ran out of the bank.

In the street, a silver Mercedes was waiting. The engine was running. The back door was open. The other two Pelottis were already inside the Mercedes, waiting impatiently for their youngest, craziest brother.

Pelottinho leaped into the Mercedes and threw the sack onto the back seat beside him. He slammed the door. The engine roared. The wheels spun. Fumes gushed out of the exhaust.

At that moment, the doors of the bank sprang open and the three security guards ran out. They drew their pistols. The Mercedes sped down the street. The three security guards started shooting.

Bam! Bam! Bam! Bam! Bam!

One bullet hit an old lady's shopping bags, puncturing a carton of orange juice. Another bullet smashed the windscreen of a lorry. Two more bullets blew out the tyres of a bus. A fifth bullet hit a statue of Emperor Pedro the Second and knocked off his nose. But not a single bullet touched the Mercedes.

Out of the back window, Pelottinho waved his arm – his one and only arm – at the security guards.

Then the Mercedes turned the corner and the Pelottis were gone.

Chapter 2

All around the Chief of Police, people were working. Police officers were interviewing the customers who had been inside the bank during the robbery. Forensics experts dusted the surfaces for fingerprints. DNA experts scraped samples into test tubes. Shoe experts squatted on the floor, drawing chalk lines around muddy footprints. Ballistics experts stuffed bullets into plastic bags. Balaclava experts inspected the black woollen mask that Pelottinho had been wearing.

The Chief of Police was a short, fat man with a round face, red cheeks and a shiny bald head. His name was Luis Gomez da Silva Mendoza Careca, but everyone called him 'sir'.

'Sir? Sir? Sir, we have the photograph, sir.'

Chief Careca stared at the junior police officer who was standing beside him. 'What did you say?'

'We've printed the photograph, sir. From the CCTV camera.' The junior officer looked nervous. His name was Detective Pereira, and he had just been promoted to the Serious Crimes Unit. This was his first week on the job. He was holding a black-and-white photo.

'Give that to me,' said Chief Careca.

'Yes, sir.'

Chief Careca grabbed the photo. He stared at the face. In a quiet voice, he whispered, 'Pelottinho.' Then he whispered the name again, very slowly, rolling every syllable around his tongue. 'Pel-lot-tin-nho. You shouldn't have come back to Rio, Pelottinho. This time, Pelottinho, things will be different. This time, Pelottinho, you will not escape me.'

The bank manager emerged from the vaults and walked slowly to the Chief of Police. He looked gloomy. He had spent the past three hours counting all the money in the vault. 'I've finished,' he said.

Chief Careca said, 'So? How much did they get?'

'A hundred and twenty-three million reais.'

Chief Careca blinked, unable to believe his ears. 'A hundred and what?'

'A hundred and twenty-three million reais,' said the bank manager. He sounded as if he could hardly believe it himself.

'Those monkeys,' muttered Chief Careca. 'Those rats. Those pigs. Are they trying to make me look like a complete idiot?'

If you're British, a hundred and twenty-three million reais is the equivalent of thirty-two million pounds. Or fifty-five million dollars if you're American. Or... well, whoever you are, and wherever you live, it's an awful lot of money.

The bank manager said, 'So, what are you going to do?'

'Do?' Chief Careca blinked. A dribble of sweat quivered on his upper lip. 'What do you think I'm going to do?'

6

'I don't have the foggiest,' said the bank manager. 'What are you going to do?'

Chief Careca's red cheeks glowed like the flames of a forest fire. He roared, 'I'm going to catch those three Pelotti brothers! And then I'm going to make them wish that they had never been born!' For the first time that day, he smiled. He rubbed his hands together, imagining all the cruel and terrible tortures that he would inflict on the three Pelotti brothers – and especially on the youngest, the wildest, the craziest, the most infuriating of them all, Felipe Pelotti, better known as Pelottinho.

A week later, on the other side of Rio de Janeiro, three men walked into a bank. They ordered everyone to lie on the floor, then forced the manager to open the vault and stuffed five brown sacks with cash. That time, the Pelotti gang got away with ninety-seven million reais.

Three days after that, the Pelottis robbed another bank in Rio. They stole eighty-eight million reais, six bags of diamonds, nine gold ingots and the salami sandwich that the bank manager had been planning to have for lunch.

Six days after that, they went back to the Banco do Brasil, and robbed it again. This time, they got away with a hundred and four million reais.

If this carried on for much longer, there wouldn't be any money left in Brazil. The Pelotti brothers would have it all.

Someone had to stop them.

But who?

Chapter 3

A zombie lurched through the tunnels. Flesh dripped from its rotting face.

The zombie opened its mouth, exposing two brown teeth and a throbbing red tongue. In a low rumbling voice, it groaned, 'Are you ready to die?'

Timothy Malt stared into the zombie's blood-red eyes and said, 'No.'

The zombie chuckled. Its mouth opened even wider. It whispered again, 'Are you ready to die?'

'I said no,' replied Tim. He pressed a button. Three high-velocity bullets fizzed from the barrel of his rifle and thumped into the middle of the zombie's chest.

'Die!' screeched the zombie in a terrifying, high-pitched voice. 'You must die!'

'Actually,' replied Tim, 'I think you must die.' He pulled the trigger again and again. The zombie screamed, toppled over and lay on the ground, not moving.

Tim grinned. He pressed SAVE so he wouldn't have to go back to the beginning of the level if another zombie got him. Then he stepped over the zombie's body and sprinted down the dark tunnel.

Grk lifted his head. His nostrils twitched.

Grk was lying on the floor in the sitting room, not far from Tim's feet. He had been lying there for about an hour, not quite asleep, but not quite awake either. The screams of zombies didn't disturb him. He could happily doze through the roar of grenade launchers and the crackle of bullets. But now, for the first time in an hour, his ears pricked up.

Without removing his eyes from the screen, Tim said, 'What is it?'

Grk didn't answer. But he sprang to his feet, ran to the window, and jumped onto a chair that gave a good view of the road. When Grk looked through the window and saw who was outside, his tail thumped on the chair's seat.

'Who is it?' said Tim.

Although he knew very well that Grk couldn't speak, he hadn't got out of the habit of talking to him. Tim had the strange sense that Grk could always understand just about anything that was said to him.

Grk barked. Grrrrwf!

If Tim had been able to speak Dog, he would have known the meaning of the word 'Grrrrwf!' Unfortunately, Tim could only speak English, a little French and a few words of Stanislavian.

Tim pressed PAUSE on the control and ambled over the window. Through the glass, he could see a thin fifteen-year-old boy walking towards the house. The boy was wearing white shorts and a white T-shirt, and carrying a tennis racket.

Grk barked again, louder. Grrrrrrrrrrrwff!

Hearing him, the boy looked up and waved. Tim waved back and Grk barked again.

'Come on,' said Tim. 'Let's open the door.'

As Tim and Grk walked to the front door, Tim wondered whether Grk had psychic powers. Was he telepathic? Could he see the future? If not, how did he always know when someone was going to arrive at the house? Why did he always lift his head and prick up his ears a few seconds before anyone came to the door?

Tim opened the door, and said, 'Hi, Max. How was practice?'

'Fine, thanks,' said Max, and walked into the house. He slotted his tennis racket into the umbrella stand, then turned round. 'I have a key, you know.'

'I know.'

'So you don't have to let me in. I could let myself in.'

'I know,' said Tim.

'So you must like letting me in?'

Tim nodded. 'I suppose I must.'

'Fine,' said Max. 'I'm going to have a shower. See you later.'

Max ran up the stairs, taking them two at a time. Tim and Grk ambled back into the sitting room. Tim sat on the sofa, pressed a button on the control to start the action, and returned to killing zombies. Grk sniffed the carpet, walked round in a circle three times, and lay down.

Apart from Tim, Max and Grk, three other people lived in the house: Mr Malt, Mrs Malt and Natascha Raffifi. Mr and Mrs Malt were Tim's parents. Both of them were working. Natascha Raffifi was Max's sister. That afternoon, just like every afternoon, she was sitting in her bedroom, reading a newspaper.

Other people read newspapers in the morning, but Natascha didn't have time. In the mornings, she was rushing from her bedroom to the bathroom, showering and dressing and cleaning her teeth. Then she was rushing downstairs, eating breakfast and putting on her shoes and going to school. She couldn't imagine how anyone could possibly have time to read a newspaper in the morning.

Natascha read the newspaper later in the day, when she came home from school. She collected the newspaper from the kitchen table, where it had been left by Mr or Mrs Malt, and carried it upstairs to her bedroom. She sat on the bed. She collected her notebook and her dictionary. She spent an hour, and sometimes more, reading the newspaper slowly and carefully from beginning to end, stopping whenever she found a word that she couldn't understand. She looked up all the difficult words in the dictionary, and wrote them down in her notebook.

Today, for instance, the front page said, 'Peace plans in jeopardy after bombing.'

Jeopardy.

Natascha stared at that word for a long time. It looked a bit like 'leopard' and a bit like 'jealousy' but neither of those would make any sense in the context.

She shook her head, and looked up 'jeopardy'. According to the dictionary, 'jeopardy' meant 'the risk of loss, harm or death'. Natascha wrote down the word and its meaning in her notebook.

In the months that she had been living with the Malts,

Natascha had filled seven notebooks. They sat in a row on the bookshelf above her bed. She didn't just write down the new English words that she had learnt. She jotted down interesting thoughts that occurred to her, and funny things that other people said, and good bits that she read in books. If she met someone who fascinated her, or did something unusual, or had a particular thought that she didn't want to forget, she wrote that down too. When Natascha grew up, she was going to be a writer, although she hadn't yet decided exactly what kind of writer. A playwright, perhaps. Or a journalist. Or perhaps even a poet.

But she wasn't planning to grow up for a long time. For now, she just wanted to learn lots of interesting new English words.

She hunched over the newspaper, and read the business pages, and the sports pages, and the arts pages, and the home news, and the foreign news. At the bottom of the page marked 'International', she saw a small paragraph with a surprising headline.

She read the headline, then read the whole paragraph.

Her face went white.

She read the paragraph again, checking that she hadn't imagined it. Then she read it again to check that she hadn't misunderstood any of the English words. Then she grabbed the newspaper, jumped off the bed, and ran through the house, shouting 'Max! Max!'

There was no answer.

She shouted louder: 'Maaaaaaaaaax!'

There was still no answer.

She ran downstairs and charged into the sitting room. Tim was squatting on the sofa, staring at the TV.

Natascha said, 'Where's Max?'

Without looking up from the TV, Tim said, 'Shower.'

'Thank you.' Natascha ran upstairs again, and tried to open the bathroom door. It was locked. Coming from the other side, she could hear the sound of running water. She hammered on the door. 'Max? Max? Are you in there?'

There was a pause, then a muffled voice said, 'What do you want?'

'Open the door.'

'I'm in the shower,' said the muffled voice.

'Then get out.'

'Why?'

'Because I have to show you something,' said Natascha.

'Can't it wait for five minutes?'

'No.'

'Just wait. I'll be out in five minutes.'

'Come on, Max. Open the door. It's important.'

'It had better be,' said the muffled voice.

Natascha waited impatiently, listening to the sounds coming from the other side. She heard water being turned off, and footsteps, and someone grumbling to himself.

The door opened. Max Raffifi looked at his sister with an impatient glare. He had a white towel tied around his waist. Water was dripping from his body to the floor, forming a small pool at his feet. He said, 'So?'

'Look,' said Natascha. She thrust the newspaper at her brother. 'Read that.'

'You got me out of the shower to read the newspaper?'

'Yes.'

'I'll read it later,' said Max. He tried to shut the door – but he couldn't, because Natascha put her foot in the way. 'Read it,' she insisted, thrusting the newspaper at her brother.

'You're very annoying,' said Max. He took the paper. His wet fingers left dark marks on the newsprint. 'What am I supposed to be reading?'

'That,' said Natascha, pointing at a paragraph at the bottom of the page marked 'International.'

Max glanced at the paragraph. He read the headline. He blinked, and leaned forward, and read the headline again. He whispered, 'I don't believe it.'

Max retreated into the bathroom, carrying the newspaper, and sat on the edge of the bath. He read the whole paragraph, then read it twice more. Natascha stood in the doorway, watching him.

When Max finished reading the paragraph for the third time, he lifted his head and looked at Natascha. He said, 'What are we going to do?'

Chapter 4

That night, just like every other night, the Malts and the Raffifis ate supper together. They had cod in white sauce, mashed potato and broad beans, followed by apple tart and vanilla ice cream.

At first, they talked about what each of them had been doing that day, but that didn't take long, because none of them had been doing anything terribly interesting.

Tim, Max and Natascha had been at school, and all their lessons had been quite boring.

Mr and Mrs Malt had been at work, which had been even more boring. Mr Malt worked as an insurance underwriter. Mrs Malt worked as a financial consultant specialising in corporate takeovers. I know some people are fascinated by insurance underwriting and financial consultancy. If you happen to be one of those people, then you're probably reading the wrong book.

Grk had been for two walks, one in the morning and one in the afternoon, and both had been extremely interesting. He had smelt the scent of a fox, and chased a squirrel, and ate half a croissant that someone had dropped in the park, and played with several different dogs – three labradors, four spaniels, two huskies and a group of multi-coloured mongrels. Unfortunately, Grk couldn't tell anyone in the room about any of these excitements. None of them could speak Dog, and he could speak nothing else. So he just lay under the table, hoping someone would drop a piece of cod on the floor, or maybe a spoonful of apple tart, or even just a broad bean.

When the Malts and the Raffifis had finished describing what had happened during the day, they discussed their plans for the weekend, and where they might go on holiday in the summer, and whether vanilla ice cream tasted of anything.

It was a perfectly normal evening.

No one noticed that Max and Natascha were unusually quiet.

Chapter 5

Tim was lying in bed. He was wearing his favourite pyjamas, a blue pair covered with pictures of hot-air balloons, and reading a book.

A piece of paper appeared in front of his book, covering the text.

Tim stared at the piece of paper. It was a paragraph torn from a newspaper. The headline read 'PELOTTI GANG STRIKES AGAIN'. Tim looked up. Max and Natascha were standing beside his bed, watching him. Tim said, 'What's this?'

'Read it,' said Natascha.

Tim said, 'Why? What's it about? Who are the Pelotti Gang?'

'Just read it,' repeated Natascha. 'You'll understand when you've read it.'

Tim felt confused, but he did as she asked. He closed his book, picked up the scrap of newspaper and started reading. This was what he read:

PELOTTI GANG STRIKES AGAIN
Rio de Janeiro has been shocked by yet another brutal bank raid by the notorious Pelotti gang. In a shoot-out, two passers-by were wounded. Both are currently in hospital. Some reports claim that both shots were fired by bank guards, not the robbers. A spokesman for the

17

bank refused to reveal how much money had been taken.

The three Pelotti brothers escaped from prison less than two months ago, but they have already robbed at least fifteen banks in the city. Some experts estimate that the Pelottis must now be among the richest men in Brazil.

Panic has spread among the citizens of Rio de Janeiro. 'I'm not leaving my money in there,' said one 83-year-old woman outside the Banco do Brasil. She had just withdrawn all her savings from the vaults. 'It's safer under my bed,' she added. 'The Pelottis won't find it there. And if they do, they'll have to kill me first.'

The Pelottis have gained an extraordinary reputation. They are daring, successful and apparently impossible to catch. The police seem unable to stop them. Local residents have called for the mayor of Rio de Janeiro to resign.

After last night's robbery, the Chief of Police, Luis Gomez da Silva Mendoza Careca, spoke to reporters. He said, 'We are on the track of the Pelottis, and we expect to arrest them within the next two or three days.' When a reporter pointed out that Chief Careca had used exactly the same words more than a month ago, Chief Careca refused to respond. For now, the banks of Rio are bracing themselves for yet more robberies.

Tim looked up and stared at Max and Natascha. 'I've read it,' he said.

'Now you understand why we have to go to Brazil,' said Natascha.

Tim stared at her in amazement. 'Brazil? What for?'

'To catch them.'

'Why?'

Natascha sighed. 'Because it is our duty. As Raffifis.'

'I'm sorry,' said Tim. 'But I don't understand. What are you talking about?'

So Natascha explained.

There were three Pelotti brothers, said Natascha. Pablo Pelotti, the eldest. José Pelotti, the middle one. And Felipe Pelotti, the youngest, who had one arm and was always called Pelottinho. Together, the three of them formed the most successful gang of criminals that Brazil had ever seen.

The Pelotti gang terrorised South America. They left a trail of murder and mayhem across Brazil, Argentina, Uruguay, Paraguay and Chile, robbing almost every bank in the region. The police despaired. Bank managers suffered nervous breakdowns. The public was furious. Newspapers demanded results. Politicians lost their jobs. But still the Pelottis continued their crimes.

And then one man managed to trap them, using little more than his own courage and intelligence. That man was Gabriel Raffifi.

'Your father,' said Tim.

Natascha nodded.

The three of them sat in silence for a minute, thinking about Gabriel Raffifi.

Natascha brushed her hair away from her face. Whenever she thought about her parents, she wanted to cry. She didn't mind crying if she was alone, but she didn't want to cry in front of Max and Tim. So she wiped her face quickly with her hands, took a deep breath, and continued with her story, explaining how Gabriel Raffifi had caught the Pelotti gang. As she described her father's intelligence and bravery, she felt so proud that she almost forgot to be sad.

Gabriel Raffifi worked as a diplomat. Several years ago, the Stanslavian Foreign Office had appointed him as the Stanislavian Ambassador to Uruguay. With his wife and their two little children, Gabriel Raffifi moved to Montevideo, the capital of Uruguay.

One hot afternoon, Gabriel Raffifi was walking through the streets when he noticed three men drinking beer in a café. They were wearing hats pulled down low over their faces and coats with the collars turned up. Something about them made him suspicious. He sat down at a nearby table, ordered a coffee and eavesdropped on their conversation.

They were speaking Portuguese. People in Uruguay speak Spanish; people in Brazil speak Portuguese. Because Gabriel Raffifi worked as a diplomat he spoke both, so he understood exactly what the men were saying. And he realised two facts.

Fact number one: the three men were Brazilian.

Fact number two: they were wearing disguises. One of them had a black beard which was attached to his chin at a wonky angle. The second had a big, floppy moustache which wobbled whenever he spoke. The third had long, blond hair that looked just like a wig. All three were wearing dark glasses. And the one with a moustache had only one arm.

Three men, thought Gabriel Raffifi. Wearing disguises. Speaking Portuguese with a Brazilian accent. And one of them only has one arm. I wonder if they are the Pelotti brothers...

Gabriel Raffifi sat there for an hour, drinking a coffee, then eating a croissant, trying to hear what the men were saying. When they paid their bill and walked away, Gabriel Raffifi followed them, taking great care to prevent them from noticing him.

He discovered where they were living. He stayed outside the house, watching the three men through the windows until he was absolutely certain that they were the Pelotti brothers. Then he fetched the police.

The Pelottis were caught and sent back to Brazil. They were tried, convicted and put in prison. Gabriel Raffifi was given a medal by the Brazilian Government and promoted by his own government, who sent him to be the Stanislavian ambassador in Latvia. From there, he was sent to Canada, then Spain and finally Britain.

When Natascha had finished telling the story of Gabriel Raffifi and the Pelotti gang, she said, 'Now you understand why we have to go to Brazil.'

'Not really,' said Tim.

'You don't?' Natascha was amazed. 'You really don't?'

'No,' said Tim. 'Sorry. But I don't.'

21

Max and Natascha glanced at one another. They both slowly shook their heads.

'Our father is dead,' said Max in a quiet voice. 'If he had been alive, he would have gone to Brazil and stopped the Pelotti brothers. He caught them last time and he would have caught them again. He can't do that. So we have to do it for him.'

'But you can't just fly to Brazil,' said Tim.

'Why not? You flew to Stanislavia. You came and rescued us from prison.'

'That was different,' said Tim.

'If you don't want to help us . . . ' Max didn't finish his sentence. He just left the words hanging in the air, then turned to Natascha, and whispered something in Stanislavian. She whispered back.

Tim always felt extremely irritated when Max and Natascha talked to one another in Stanislavian. He couldn't understand what they were saying – he could only speak a few words of their language – and he knew that they would be saying something that they didn't want him to hear. So he interrupted. 'Of course I want to help you,' he said. 'What shall I do?'

At two o'clock in the morning, Tim tiptoed out of his bedroom. The house was quiet. He walked slowly past his parents' bedroom, and padded down the stairs to the hallway. He found his father's jacket, hanging from a hook near the front door. Reaching into the jacket, he fished out his father's wallet.

Tim knew what he was doing was wrong. He knew

22

that using his father's credit card wasn't really different from stealing money from his father's wallet, even if it felt completely different because the crisp banknotes never actually touched his fingers. He knew that he should walk into his parents' bedroom, and wake them, and ask them what to do.

But he put all these thoughts to one side. If Max and Natascha needed his help, then he would help them. It was as simple as that.

In the sitting room, the computer was humming gently to itself. Tim sat down. He connected to a website that sold tickets. He found a flight from London to Rio de Janeiro.

There was a box saying: 'Number of passengers'.

Tim typed '2'.

Before completing the rest of the details on the form, Tim stared at the screen for a minute. He thought about his parents, lying upstairs in their bed, snoring peacefully. He thought about Grk, curled up on the mat by the front door, protecting the house from burglars. He thought about Max and Natascha, sitting on the bed upstairs.

He tried to imagine how he would feel tomorrow, sitting alone in the house, knowing that Max and Natascha were in Brazil.

He moved the mouse across the screen, and returned to the box marked 'Number of passengers'.

He deleted '2' and typed '4'.

Chapter 6

When Mr and Mrs Malt had gone to work, and Tim and Natascha and Max had gone to school, Grk was alone in the house.

He lay down on the carpet with his head on his paws and stared through the French windows.

Usually, he would stay there for the whole day.

He might go downstairs to the kitchen and drink a little water.

If someone came to the front door, he might bark at them, just to let them know that burglars were not welcome at this particular house.

If any letters or parcels dropped through the letter box, he would sniff the envelopes. You never know: maybe one would contain some food. A steak, perhaps. Or a chicken leg. Perhaps a lamb chop or some bacon. Grk hadn't yet found food in an envelope, but he wasn't the type of dog who gave up easily.

When he wasn't drinking water or barking at burglars or sniffing envelopes, Grk mostly lay on the carpet in the sitting room, staring through the French windows, watching for squirrels and cats. He usually spent the whole day there, waiting for someone to come home and take him for a walk.

Today, things were different.

Grk had been lying down for about half an hour when

he heard footsteps, walking up the stairs that led to the front door. He heard a key turning in the lock. He saw the door open. Then he leaped forward, his tail wagging, his eyes wide open with excitement, and threw himself at the three people who walked into the house. Grk didn't understand why Max, Natascha and Tim had come home eight hours early. But he knew this much: he was overjoyed to see them.

All three children hurried upstairs to their bedrooms. Grk sat at the bottom of the staircase, waiting for them. Five minutes later, they returned. Each of them was carrying a bag.

Tim fixed a lead to Grk's collar. He glanced at his bag and wondered if he had forgotten anything. He felt nervous.

Max said, 'Maybe Grk should stay here.'

Tim and Natascha both stared at him in amazement. 'Leave Grk?' said Tim. 'But why?'

'He might cause problems.'

'He won't cause any problems,' said Natascha. 'He'll help us. He'll probably be more useful than you.'

'Ha ha,' said Max.

Natascha pretended not to hear him. She turned to Tim. 'What do you think? Shall we leave Max behind?'

Tim didn't want to get involved in any squabbles between the two siblings. So he just said, 'Hold this.' He thrust Grk's lead into Natascha's hand, and ran downstairs to the kitchen. He found a piece of paper and a pen, and scrawled a quick note.

Dear Mum and Dad,
I'm really sorry, but I've had to go somewhere with Max and Natascha and Grk.
They need my help.
Please don't be upset.
We'll be back soon. I promise.
Loads of love from Tim

He placed the note in the middle of the kitchen table where it couldn't be missed. He ran upstairs again. Together, the three children and Grk walked out of the house.

Chapter 7

There are only two ways to sleep on an aeroplane.

The first way is to fly first class.

In first class, the seats are tall and wide and padded. You can stretch your legs. You get lots of cushions for your head. You can snooze in comfort.

The second way to sleep on an aeroplane is to be a small dog.

If you are a small dog, you can curl up comfortably on a narrow, cramped chair. Your head won't keep banging against the window. Your legs won't get stuck under the chair in front. You won't be woken up by your neighbour's knees or elbows. You can snooze in comfort.

Unfortunately, Timothy Malt, Max Raffifi and Natascha Raffifi were not small dogs. Nor were they flying first class. Which meant that, on the twelve-hour flight from London to Rio de Janeiro, only Grk slept properly.

When they arrived in Rio, Tim, Natascha and Max felt utterly exhausted. As they emerged from the plane, the heat wrapped around them like a blanket. Sunlight glared off every surface. The three children covered their eyes with their hands. All they wanted was to go to bed for a long, long time.

Grk strained on his lead and sniffed the air, thrilled by

all the new and unusual scents he could smell. All he wanted was to sprint around the city, sniffing lampposts and trees, peeing everywhere, letting the local dogs know that he had arrived.

'Slow down,' said Tim, tugging Grk's lead. 'Hey! Don't pull me down the stairs!'

Grk took no notice. He was too excited. He sprinted down the stairs, pulling Tim after him. When they got to the bottom, Grk ran round the corner to one of the aeroplane's huge wheels. He lifted his back leg, and had a long, satisfying pee against the rubber tyre.

Tim looked the other way, pretending that he had no idea what Grk was doing.

As a large pool of dog pee spread across the tarmac, Tim and Grk hurried away to find Max and Natascha. When the four of them were reunited, they joined the queue of passengers heading for the terminal.

Two police officers were standing on either side of the glass doors that led into the airport. They watched all the passengers who walked past. Natascha smiled at the policemen. '*Bom dia*,' she said.

'*Bom dia*,' replied the nearest policeman.

Tim and Max stared at Natascha in amazement. Tim said, 'What did that mean?'

'I've been learning some Portuguese,' explained Natascha. '"*Bom dia*" means "good morning".'

Max said, 'What else have you learnt?'

'*Pão. Leite. Queijo.*' replied Natascha. 'Those are the words for bread, milk and cheese. So if we find a café, we could have some breakfast.'

28

That sounded like a good plan to Max and Tim. They both quickened their step and hurried towards the passport booth.

There was a long queue which shuffled forwards very slowly. One by one, the passengers went through passport control. A small bald man with a twirly moustache sat in the booth, checking everyone's passports.

It was Tim's turn. '*Bom dia*,' said Tim, and handed his passport to the bald man.

The bald man stared at Tim and did not reply.

'*Bom dia*,' said Tim for a second time.

Without saying a word, the bald man opened Tim's passport, and stared for a long time at the photograph. He lifted his head and looked at Tim. Finally, in a quiet voice, he said, 'Tell me. Your name is what?'

'Timothy Malt.'

'Timothy Malt,' repeated the bald man. 'From London?'

'Yes.'

'And tell me, Timothy Malt, do you travel to Brazil alone with yourself?'

'No,' replied Tim. 'I'm travelling with them.' Tim turned and pointed at Max and Natascha, who were waiting at the front of the queue, holding their passports in their hands. 'And him,' said Tim, pointing at Grk.

'Tell me, what are their names, please?'

'Their names are Max and Natascha Raffifi. And his name is Grk.'

'Natascha Raffifi and Max Raffifi and Timothy Malt.'

'And Grk,' said Tim.

The bald man nodded. He beckoned to the Raffifis and called, 'Please! You will come here!'

Max and Natascha did as they were told.

'This way,' said the bald man. 'Over here. Follow me, please.'

Together, the bald man led them through the airport to a door marked ENTRADA PROIBIDA. Two policemen were standing by the door. They had blue uniforms with silver buttons. The bald man spoke to the policemen in Portuguese. One of them nodded and opened the door.

'In here, please,' said the bald man.

They went through the door and walked down a long, narrow corridor.

Tim tugged the bald man's sleeve. 'Where are you taking us?'

'Please, no talking,' replied the bald man.

'I am a British citizen,' said Tim, trying to sound as stern and adult as possible. 'You have no right to treat me like this.'

The bald man smiled as if Tim had said something quite funny, and kept walking.

A minute later, they reached another door, guarded by two more policemen. The bald man spoke to them in Portuguese, and they immediately opened the door. It was an exit to a private car park at the back of the airport. A police car was waiting with its engine running.

The bald man opened the car's back door and ushered the children onto the back seat, followed by Grk.

'Enjoy your stay in Brazil,' said the bald man. He

slammed the door. The driver started the engine and they drove out of the airport. They joined a busy main road and headed towards the centre of Rio de Janeiro.

A thin man in a police uniform was sitting in the passenger seat. He turned round and smiled at the three children. 'Hello, Max and Natascha,' he said. 'Hello, Tim.'

The children stared at the thin man, surprised that he knew their names. None of them had ever seen him before.

The thin man said, 'And hello to you too, Grk. It is a great pleasure to meet you.'

Grk didn't even look up. He was busy, sniffing the car's back seat, following the smells of the last few people to sit here.

The thin man said, 'On behalf of the government of Brazil and the city of Rio de Janeiro, I would like to welcome you to Brazil. We are very proud to have the children of Gabriel Raffifi as our guests.'

Max and Natascha stared at the thin man in amazement. His mention of their father shocked them into silence.

Tim was the first to speak. 'If you don't mind me asking, where are you taking us?'

'To the Copacabana Castle,' said the thin man.

'Where?'

'The Copacabana Castle.'

'Where's that?'

'Where you will be staying.' The thin man smiled. 'It is a very good hotel. You will like it. Chief Careca has

31

booked one of the very best suites for you. By the way, Chief Careca sends his apologies. If he was not so busy, he would be here himself. But he will come to meet you tomorrow morning. For breakfast. When you have had a chance to sleep properly. Now, please, sit back. Enjoy the ride. Enjoy the view. Welcome to Rio.'

Chapter 8

It is universally agreed that the Copacabana Castle is the best hotel in Rio de Janeiro. There are even those who claim that the Copacabana Castle is the best hotel in the entire world. When famous film stars visit Rio, they wouldn't stay anywhere else. The same goes for presidents, princesses, pop stars and millionaires of all shapes and sizes.

You can get whatever you want in the Copacabana Castle. You can eat, sleep, dance and shop. You can tone your muscles or broaden your mind. You can meet and greet. You can surf and turf. You can polish your nails or shine your shoes. If a guest of the Copacabana Castle wants anything, he or she just needs to click his or her fingers – or pick up the pink telephone in his or her room – and it will be found.

The Copacabana Castle has two gyms, three swimming pools and five tennis courts. There are four restaurants and six bars. Guests are also offered the use of a sauna, a casino, a crèche, a bookshop, a library, a cinema, a conference hall and a banquet suite.

When Tim, Max and Natascha reached the Copacabana Castle, they didn't stop to eat in any of the restaurants or order a drink in any of the bars. They didn't dip their toes into the pools or tour the glistening machines that filled the gyms. They avoided the tennis courts and the casino and the sauna. No, they just hurried upstairs to their suite, cleaned their teeth, slid between the crisp white sheets of their beds, and fell asleep.

A few hours later, Mr and Mrs Malt arrived in Rio. They took a taxi from the airport to the hotel and tiptoed into the suite, taking care not to wake the children. Then they went to bed too.

The previous day, when Tim hadn't arrived at school, his teacher waited for a few minutes, thinking that he must have been delayed by a traffic jam or a doctor's appointment. After an hour, she began to worry that something was seriously wrong. She sent a message to the headmistress, who rang Mrs Malt. 'I'm terribly sorry to bother you,' said Tim's headmistress. 'But Tim didn't come to school today. I thought we should let you know. He's not ill, is he?'

'No, no, he's not,' said Mrs Malt. 'Thank you for letting me know.' She put the phone down, feeling a little worried. She wondered what she should do. Would it be better to wait a little? Or should she leave the office immediately?

Before she could make a decision, her phone rang for a second time. It was the headmistress again. 'I'm terribly sorry to keep bothering you,' said the headmistress. 'But I've got some rather worrying news. Natascha didn't come to school either.'

Now Mrs Malt was very worried. She decided to leave the office, hurry home and see if she could find any trace of Tim or Natascha.

34

As Mrs Malt walked briskly down the corridor to the lift, her mobile phone rang. It was Max's headmaster, asking why Max hadn't arrived at school.

Mrs Malt panicked. She rang her husband. He panicked too. They both left their offices and drove home. In the kitchen, they found Tim's note.

Mr and Mrs Malt rang the credit card company, then the airport, and quickly discovered what had happened.

Mrs Malt rang the British Embassy in Brazil, and asked them to inform the Brazilian authorities that Tim, Natascha, Max and Grk would soon be arriving at Rio airport. The Ambassador informed the Brazilian police and immigration authorities, who promised to detain the children when they arrived.

Mr and Mrs Malt packed their suitcases and left the house. At the airport, they rushed to the front of all the queues and boarded the next flight to Brazil.

Chapter 9

'It is a great honour to meet you,' said Chief Careca. He shook hands with Max, then with Natascha, and then with Max again. 'I am most happily honoured.'

'Thank you,' said Natascha.

'We are very pleased to meet you too,' said Max.

'No, no,' said Chief Careca. 'To meet me, yes, perhaps this is nice. But to meet the children of Gabriel Raffifi – this is the greatest honour. Your father was a hero. You must be very proud of him.'

Max and Natascha nodded. Both of them agreed that they were very proud of their father. Natascha brushed the stray hairs away from her face. Max looked over the edge of the balcony and stared at the sea. For a minute, no one spoke.

Mrs Malt picked up the coffee jug. 'Will you have a drop of coffee?'

'Thank you,' replied Chief Careca. 'That would be most kind.'

'The coffee is delicious,' said Mrs Malt.

'Of course.' Chief Careca nodded. 'In Brazil, we grow the best coffee in the world.'

'So I've heard,' said Mrs Malt. She filled Chief Careca's cup, then pushed the milk jug across the table to him.

They were sitting on the wide balcony that ran

alongside their suite. The view was extraordinarily beautiful, looking across the wide expanse of Copacabana Beach to the glistening turquoise ocean and the mountains that circled the bay. Down on the beach, people were sunbathing or swimming or playing football on the sand.

The sun was hot and the sky was blue and the table was set with a magnificent breakfast. After a glass of orange juice, each of them was served with a plate of succulent fruits, so fresh that they might just have dropped from the tree. Then they had warm croissants and sweet pastries and *pão de queijo*, a Brazilian speciality, little cheese rolls which are deliciously squidgy.

When Chief Careca had discovered that the son and daughter of Gabriel Raffifi had arrived in Rio de Janeiro, he wanted to thank them in some way for their father's actions. So he booked the Malts, the Raffifis and Grk into the best suite in the city's finest hotel, all paid for by the police department.

But he also wanted them to be completely safe. The Pelotti brothers hated the very name 'Raffifi' and would have given anything to take revenge on the Raffifi family. So Chief Careca arranged for a squad of experienced police officers to guard the Raffifis twenty-four hours a day. 'The Pelottis are the most dangerous men in Brazil,' explained Chief Careca. 'They are cunning, ruthless and utterly brutal. They kill without even thinking. Like this!' He slapped his fist on the table. The coffee cups jumped. So did everyone else around the table. Chief Careca didn't seem to notice.

'Like you or me would kill a mosquito, they kill a human being. But they are not stupid. Oh no, they are very different from stupid. If they see you are guarded by many police, many guns, they will not attack you. You will be safe here.'

Tim said, 'Why would they want to attack us?'

'Not you, Timothy Malt.' Chief Careca shook his head. 'They do not care about you.'

Tim felt a bit disappointed. Why didn't they care about him? Wasn't he good enough for them?

'But you...' Chief Careca waved his arm at Max and Natascha. 'The Pelottis certainly care about you. They want revenge. You understand? For the actions of your father. They hate your father for what he did. And so they hate you too.' Chief Careca smiled. 'But there is no need to worry. You are in safe hands. You can stay here in comfort, and enjoy the delights of Rio, which is the most beautiful city on the planet. You can have the best holiday of your lives.'

'We don't want a holiday,' said Max. 'We want to catch the Pelottis.'

'We want to help,' added Natascha.

Chief Careca smiled again. 'The three of you have travelled from London...'

'Four,' interrupted Natascha.

'Oh, I am sorry. The three of you and your excellent dog.'

Grk knew that they were talking about him. He lifted his head and looked around. But when he realised that there was no food involved, he went back to sleep.

'The four of you have travelled from London to Rio,' said Chief Careca. 'You are obviously unusual children. And you have a very unusual dog. But this does not mean that you can capture the Pelotti brothers.'

'What about an ambush?' suggested Max. 'If they want to kill us, like you say, they'll come and find us. Then you could ambush them.'

Chief Careca shook his head. 'The Pelottis are the most dangerous criminals that I have encountered in thirty-two years as a police officer. They are cruel. They are violent. They are ruthless. But they are not stupid. They would guess we were planning to ambush them.'

Natascha sighed. 'There must be some way we could help.'

'Your father was one of the most clever and most brave men that I have ever met,' said Chief Careca. 'I am sure that the two of you are just as clever and just as brave. And one day, you will do great things with your lives, just as he did. But now... How old are you?'

'Twelve,' said Natascha.

'I'm fifteen,' said Max.

Chief Careca nodded. 'You are children. Yes, you are brave, and yes, you are clever, like your father. But you are just children. Twelve and fifteen. This is children.' He sighed and stared over the balcony at the ocean. When he next spoke, Chief Careca sounded weary, and perhaps even depressed. 'I have been searching for the Pelotti brothers for two months. I have hundreds of men and women working for me. I have computers and cameras and cars. I have fingerprint experts and forensics experts and DNA experts. If I can't catch the Pelotti brothers, do you really think that you could?'

Max and Natascha glanced at one another. They spoke quickly and earnestly in Stanislavian. No one else could understand what they were saying. Finally, they reached an agreement. They looked back at Chief Careca. Max said, 'You are right. We would not be able to find the Pelottis.'

Chief Careca smiled, pleased that they were being so sensible. 'However, I thought you might be interested to see this.' He reached into his pocket, and pulled out a transparent plastic bag. Inside, there was a piece of black cloth. He held it up so everyone could see. 'Do you know what this is? Can you guess?'

Grk hurried forwards, and lifted his head, and poked his nose at the plastic bag. Perhaps he thought it was something to eat.

'Go on,' said Chief Careca. 'You smell it.' He thrust the black cloth at Grk's nose.

Grk took several long, deep sniffs.

Chief Careca said, 'Do you know what this is?'

Grk didn't respond. He didn't even look up. He just continued sniffing.

Chief Careca smiled. 'If you ever smell the man who owns that smell, you tell us. You understand, little dog? Because there is a big reward for whoever finds that man.'

Max said, 'I know what that is.' The others turned to look at him. Max continued, 'That's a mask, isn't it? A mask that belongs to one of the robbers.'

Chief Careca nodded. 'Precisely. This is the mask that

Pelottinho wore. He dropped it on the floor after the first of the robberies. Since then, he has never bothered wearing a mask. We know who he is. He knows we know who he is. So he does not need to disguise himself.'

He threw the mask on the table. They all stared at it.

Grk's nostrils twitched once more. He was storing the smell of that mask, keeping it deep inside his memory.

After breakfast, Chief Careca took Max and Natascha on a tour of Rio de Janeiro.

Rio de Janeiro is one of the most beautiful cities on the planet. Having flown so far, it would have been ridiculous to turn round and go straight home again without seeing any of the sights. So Mr and Mrs Malt accepted Chief Careca's invitation to stay in the suite for a few days. The Malts, the Raffifis and Grk would stay in the Copacabana Castle until the weekend, then fly back to London in time to go to school and work on Monday morning.

Chief Careca invited Tim to join them on the tour, but Mr and Mrs Malt refused on Tim's behalf. They explained that Tim would prefer to spend the day in the hotel with them.

That wasn't true. Tim would have loved to go on the tour.

The real reason was that Mr and Mrs Malt didn't want to let Tim out of their sight. His disappearance had shocked them terribly. They didn't want any opportunity for him to disappear again. So, they wanted to stay right beside him for every minute of their stay in Brazil.

No one asked Tim what he would like to do.

No one asked Grk either.

Chief Careca led Max and Natascha downstairs to the lobby. The three of them emerged from the grand entrance of the Copacabana Castle, and climbed into the waiting limousine. The chauffeur tipped his hat at them. The limousine pulled away from the kerb and drove quickly through the streets of Rio. Three police motorbikes drove ahead. Two police vans and five more motorbikes drove behind. Chief Careca wasn't taking any chances. If the Pelotti brothers tried to ambush the Raffifis, they would have to fight their way through thirty armed police.

On their tour of the city, Max and Natascha drove the whole length of Copacabana Beach. They saw the Corcovado mountain with the enormous statue of Jesus Christ, which stands overlooking the city with his arms outstretched. They took a cable car to the top of the Pão de Açucar – the Sugar Loaf Mountain – and saw the amazing views over the bay.

From the Pão de Açucar, they went to Ipanema, one of the smartest districts in Rio. They shopped for clothes and CDs, then walked down to the beach. Six policemen hurried after them – one carrying their towels, another holding a walkie-talkie and the final four keeping their eyes peeled for the Pelottis.

After a quick swim in the sea, Max and Natascha ate lunch in the café where Antonio Carlos Jobim and Vinicius de Moraes wrote Rio's most famous song, 'The Girl from Ipanema'.

'I like this city,' said Natascha.

'Me too.' Max leaned back in his chair and put his hands behind his head. 'It's really cool.'

'When I grow up, I might come and live here.'

'I'd rather live in Stanislavia,' said Max. 'But I'll definitely come and visit you.'

They sat in silence for a moment. Then Max said, 'What about the Pelottis? Do you think we should be looking for them?'

'I wish we could,' replied Natascha. 'But I don't know how. Or where. Do you?'

Max shook his head slowly. 'I was thinking about Dad. When he found the Pelottis, he wasn't looking for them. He just happened to sit at the next table in a café. It was luck.'

'Maybe we'll be lucky too,' said Natascha.

'Maybe,' said Max. He picked up his glass and drank the last drops of pineapple juice. Then he looked around, hoping that he might spot three men wearing false wigs, fake moustaches and dark glasses. But he couldn't see anyone except the waiters who worked in the café and the policemen who were guarding him and Natascha.

Chapter 10

Tim was learning the names of unusual fruit.

In the hotel suite, a big bowl packed with fruit stood on the sideboard. Pineapples, oranges, apples, grapes, peaches and mangos sat in the bowl alongside all kinds of oddly-shaped fruit that Tim had never seen until yesterday. He had been learning the names of these new fruit. That was papaya. This was guava and that was a cumquat. And that one... it was called something like 'pow pow'.

Tim sighed. Learning the names of exotic fruit was quite fun – but it wasn't enough fun for a whole day.

The suite was huge. It had seven rooms. There were three bedrooms, three bathrooms and a massive sitting room with two long leather sofas. A flatscreen TV with a 42-inch screen was screwed to one wall.

Tim stood in the middle of the suite, stared at the sofas, the TV and the basket of fruit, and wished that he was anywhere but here.

He went onto the balcony. Mr and Mrs Malt were lying in deckchairs, reading their books, tanning themselves in the hot sun. Tim said, 'Dad?'

'Uh-huh,' said Mr Malt, without looking up from his book. He was reading *A Guide to the Economy and Infrastructure of Brazil – Volume Three*.

Tim said, 'Can I go for a walk?'

'No.'

'Why not?'

'We've already talked about this,' said Mr Malt. He picked up a pencil and underlined a sentence in the book. Then he continued reading.

For a minute or two, no one spoke.

Then Tim said, 'Mum?'

'Hmmm,' replied Mrs Malt, without looking up from her book. She was reading *The Alchemist*.

Tim said, 'Grk needs a pee.'

'Ring room service,' said Mrs Malt. 'Press star, then 101. They'll send a dog walker.'

'I could walk him,' said Tim. 'I could take him round the block.'

'Round the block?' said Mrs Malt. She laughed. 'Did you hear that, Terence? Tim wants to go for a walk around the block.'

Mr Malt shook his head in astonishment. He looked at Tim. 'Don't you know where we are?'

'Of course I do,' said Tim. 'We're in Rio de Janeiro.'

'Which just happens be one of the most dangerous cities on the planet. Out there . . . ' Mr Malt waved his arm, gesturing at everything that lay on the other side of the balcony. 'You wouldn't last five minutes, Tim. It's nothing but guns and knives and drugs and criminals. This isn't like home. You can't just walk round the block. Do you understand?'

'Yes, Dad,' said Tim.

'Wait till tomorrow,' said Mr Malt. 'When your mother and I have recovered from the flight. We'll have more energy. And all of us will go on a tour of the city. All right?'

'Yes, Dad,' said Tim with a sigh. He turned round and walked slowly back into the suite. Grk hurried after him.

Chapter 11

In the afternoon, Max and Natascha went to the Maracanã Stadium, the largest football stadium in the world. Built for the World Cup Finals in 1950, the Maracanã has enough seats to hold two hundred thousand people.

When Max and Natascha got to the stadium, they were led through the players' entrance and across the pitch to one of the goals. Chief Careca had arranged for Dida to come and meet them. Dida was the goalkeeper for the Brazilian team.

Dida shook hands with each of them. Then he lined up ten footballs opposite the goal, and invited Max and Natascha to try and score a penalty against him. Max went first. He booted the ball towards the goal. Dida dived to his left. His fingers scraped the ball, and he tipped it around the post.

'Brazil: one. Raffifis: nil,' said Dida with a big toothy smile. He pointed at Natascha. 'Now, you.'

Natascha placed the ball on the penalty spot and took a couple of steps backwards. She ran up to the ball and kicked it as hard as she could.

Dida dived the wrong way. The ball thumped into the back of the net.

'One-all,' said Dida.

Natascha couldn't stop grinning.

It was Max's turn. He placed the third ball on the penalty spot and took a long, hard look at Dida, trying to guess which way he would dive.

Tim walked out of the suite and wandered along the balcony. Mr Malt was slumped in a deckchair, and Mrs Malt was lying on a towel. Both of them were wearing sunhats and sunglasses. Their faces, arms and necks were smothered in suntan lotion. Mrs Malt had almost finished *The Alchemist*. Mr Malt was reading *A Guide to the Economy and Infrastructure of Brazil – Volume Four*. Neither of them looked up when Tim emerged onto the balcony.

Tim stared at his parents for a minute. He said, 'I'm bored.'

Neither of them responded.

So Tim said it again, louder. 'I'm bored.'

'Read a book,' replied Mrs Malt.

'I've read all my books,' said Tim.

'Then play a game.'

'I don't have any games.'

Mr and Mrs Malt didn't say anything. They carried on reading.

Tim said, 'Can I go for a walk?'

'No,' said Mrs Malt.

'Why not?'

Mrs Malt sighed. She said, 'Terence?'

'Yes, dear,' replied Mr Malt.

'You talk to Tim.'

'Yes, dear,' said Mr Malt. He closed his book, and

looked at Tim. 'Now, Tim. We've already discussed this. You can't just walk around Rio. It's not that sort of place.'

Tim said, 'But...'

'No buts,' said Mr Malt, shaking his head from side to side. 'This is one of the most dangerous cities on the planet. As soon as you walk out of the door, you'll be attacked by muggers. Do you really think we're going to let that happen? Do you think we'd let you wander around a city like this?'

Tim shrugged his shoulders. 'Maybe.'

'Absolutely not,' said Mr Malt. 'So sit down, read a book and be patient. Just enjoy staying in this lovely hotel. Enjoy the sunshine. Tomorrow, when your mother and I have recovered from the extremely long flight that we've just endured, we'll take you on a tour of the city. All right?'

'S'pose so,' said Tim. He padded gloomily back inside the suite, sat on the sofa and switched on the TV.

An hour later, Tim walked over to the window, and looked outside.

On the balcony, Tim's parents were slumped in their deckchairs. Mr Malt's eyes were shut and his mouth was open. He was snoring gently to himself. His copy of *A Guide to the Economy and Infrastructure of Brazil – Volume Five* lay on the floor at his feet. The book must have fallen from his hands when he nodded off. Mrs Malt was asleep too. She had a white hat over her face. Her arms were hanging limply by her sides.

49

As Tim stared at his parents, he had an idea.

Just a little idea.

The type of idea that made him smile.

He turned round. On the other side of the room, Grk was lying on the floor, his eyes half-closed. Tim whistled gently. Grk lifted his head.

Tim whispered, 'Walk?'

Grk's tail wagged. He barked excitedly.

'Shhh!' whispered Tim, putting his finger to his lips. He turned round and stared through the window.

On the balcony, Mrs Malt lifted her head, woken by Grk's bark. She blinked. She yawned. She shut her eyes, put her head down and went back to sleep.

Tim waited for a moment, but his mother didn't move again.

'Come on,' hissed Tim. 'Let's go.' He padded across the thick carpet to the door. Grk bounded after him. Tim opened the door and they stepped outside. In the corridor, Tim looked to the right, and then to the left. All the doors were shut. Tim could hear voices coming from somewhere, but couldn't see any people. There had been several policemen guarding the corridor when Max and Natascha were inside the suite, but they had gone with the Raffifis. No one had stayed behind to guard the Malts.

Slowly, silently, Tim closed the door and tugged Grk's lead. They walked down the corridor and stood opposite the lift. Tim pressed the button to summon it.

PING! The lift arrived. The door slid open. Tim and Grk stepped inside.

In the lift, a small man was sitting on a tall stool. He had a wrinkled, leathery face, and he was wearing a red uniform. He said something in Portuguese.

Tim shook his head. 'Do you speak English?'

'Oh, yes,' replied the man. 'Very good English. What floor is you want?'

'Downstairs,' said Tim. 'We want to go outside.'

'Ground floor, coming down!' The leathery-faced man pressed a button. The doors slid shut. The lift descended.

When the doors opened again, Tim and Grk stepped into the lobby. Porters were hurrying past, carrying bags and suitcases. Tourists jabbered to one another in a multitude of languages. Tim and Grk walked through the crowd to the big glass doors. The doorman tipped his top hat. '*Boa tarde*,' he said. 'Good afternoon.'

'Good afternoon,' replied Tim.

'Taxi? You want taxi?'

'No, thanks,' said Tim. 'I'd rather walk.'

Grk started sniffing the doorman's shiny shoes. Tim knew what would happen next: Grk would lift his leg and pee on the black shiny leather. To stop that happening, Tim tugged the lead, pulling Grk away from the doorman's shoe, and they walked briskly through the big glass doors into the streets of Rio de Janeiro.

Chapter 12

Tim had no idea where he was going. Nor did he know what he was looking for. Perhaps he wasn't even looking for anything. He just wanted to see the city for himself.

Until now, he had only seen the city from a distance. He had stared through the window of a car. He had gazed down from the balcony of the hotel room. It had been like seeing a city on television. You see it, but you don't feel it. You can't touch it or smell it.

As Tim and Grk walked away from the hotel and dipped into the streets of Rio de Janeiro, they finally saw the city for themselves. They felt it. They smelt it. They touched it. And the city overwhelmed them with smells and sights and feelings.

Tim only knew one city really well. That was London, the place that he had been born and the place that he had always lived.

But perhaps he didn't even know London very well. Thinking about it, he realised that he had never properly walked through London. Just about every day, he walked round the block with Grk. At weekends, they strolled through the park. Often, he went to or from school alone. But he had never just wandered through the city, looking at the buildings and observing the people and watching how things worked.

Walking into Rio, Tim didn't know which way to go, and he didn't particularly care. At every crossroads, he let Grk choose their direction.

Grk knew exactly where he wanted to go. He followed interesting smells on the pavement. He darted from lamppost to tree, sniffing and snuffling, rubbing the earth with his nose, discovering things. Every now and then, Grk lifted his leg, and peed. Tim followed him, pulled by Grk's lead.

They walked slowly. While Grk sniffed and peed, Tim looked at everything. He stared at the houses, the cars, the birds, the trees, the people . . .

He watched women in bikinis walking down the street, carrying their bags from the supermarket.

He stared through the windows of shops selling everything from knives to cheese, shoes to paintings.

He gazed up at elegant buildings with tall windows and long balconies. Right at the top, Brazilian flags waved in the breeze. Tim recognised the colours and the pattern of the Brazilian flag: it was a green rectangle surrounding a yellow diamond. In the middle of the yellow diamond, there was a blue circle, spattered with stars. A white banner ran across the middle of the circle. Three words were written on the banner: 'ORDEM E PROGRESSO.' Yesterday, Mr Malt had told Tim what the three words meant: 'Order and Progress.' He had also explained that there were twenty-seven stars on the flag, one for each state in Brazil.

Wherever he went, Tim saw the Brazilian flag. Brazilians were obviously very proud of being

Brazilian. They posted the flag in their windows, and stuck it to their cars, and wore it on their T-shirts.

He stood outside a restaurant, and sniffed the air, and smelt the delicious scents coming from the kitchens. He began to feel a little hungry. He also felt envious of Grk, who burrowed around in the restaurant's dustbins and emerged carrying a big bone. Tim let Grk chew on the bone for a few minutes, then persuaded him to drop it, and they continued walking.

Tim watched a boy bouncing a football on his head.

He watched an argument between two men. They stood on opposite sides of a busy road, shouting at one another across the traffic.

This would never get boring, thought Tim. I could spend my whole life here, looking at things.

The hot sun burnt Tim's skin, so he tried to stay in the shade as much as possible. He felt thirsty. Whenever they passed a puddle, Grk lapped up a few sips of water. Tim envied him.

By the side of the road, people were selling big round green coconuts. They chopped off the end of the coconut with a machete, then popped a straw through the hole, so you could drink the coconut juice. It looked delicious, but Tim didn't have any money.

Once, a woman almost tripped over Grk's lead. She turned round and yelled at Tim. He had no idea what she was saying, so he just muttered, 'I'm sorry. I'm very sorry. I didn't do it on purpose.' The woman shouted at him again, and hurried away.

Tim soon forgot her. There was so much to see, he didn't have space in his mind to worry about silly women. He hurried onwards, down one street, then another, never looking back.

Tim wasn't wearing a watch. He didn't know how long he had been walking. But he suddenly noticed that the sky had darkened. The sun had set. It would be night soon.

He looked around. The streets were unfamiliar. He couldn't read any of the signs, because they were in Portuguese. Which way had he come? Down that street? Or that one? He had no idea.

Tim realised something rather surprising.

He was lost.

He stared at the people hurrying past. He wanted to stop someone and ask them how to get back to the hotel. But who should he ask? Would any of them speak English? And would they help him?

Tim wondered if he had been a bit stupid. Should he have told someone where he was going? Should he have brought some money? If he had some money, he could get into a taxi, and say to the driver: 'Take me to the Copacabana Castle.'

But he was lost in the middle of a strange city with no money and no idea where to go.

He wondered what to do.

He looked around, hoping to see a policeman or a traffic warden. Who could he ask? Who would help him? He stared at the drivers in their cars and the pedestrians hurrying along the pavement, and wondered whether any of them would help him.

Tim felt small.

Of course, there was one very simple reason why he felt like that: he was small. Most of the time, he liked being small. He saw the world in a different way from adults. He noticed different things. He was closer to the ground. Often, when Tim was walking with his parents, he saw things that they had missed. He saw a coin glittering in the road. Or he saw a piece of paper stuck between two paving stones. Or he saw a little brown rat squeezing between a gap in the bricks of an old house.

But being small isn't always an advantage. Surrounded by all these people, hurrying home, rushing through the streets, Tim felt small and weak and ignored and helpless.

He looked around, staring up and down the street, hoping to see someone who might help.

Further down the street, a small boy was sitting on some steps. The boy was about the same age as Tim. He had thin arms and black hair. He was wearing dirty shorts and an even dirtier T-shirt. The small boy was watching the crowd hurry past. He didn't seem to have anywhere to go.

'Come on.' Tim tugged Grk's lead. 'This way.'

Tim and Grk hurried along the pavement. A businessman bumped into Tim, knocking him sideways, and didn't even pause to apologise. Tim shook his head. Why were people so rude?

They reached the boy. Tim said, 'Hi.'

The boy looked up and stared at him without replying.

Tim said, 'Can you help me? I want to find the Copacabana Castle. Do you know where it is?'

The boy said something that Tim couldn't understand.

'I'm sorry, I don't speak Portuguese,' said Tim. 'Do you speak English?'

The boy said something else that Tim couldn't understand, then turned and lifted his hand to his mouth. He made the loudest whistle that Tim had ever heard. On the other side of the street, another boy swivelled his head. He stared at them for a second, then ran across the street, not even glancing at the cars. Angry drivers tooted their horns and swerved to avoid him.

The two boys chattered. Both of them were roughly the same age as Tim, probably eleven or twelve years old, but they were smaller and thinner than him. They looked as if they didn't eat often. Through their skin, you could see the shape of their bones. They both wore old clothes. Neither of them had shoes, just tatty flip-flops. Their toes were bruised and grubby.

The second boy turned to Tim. 'You American? Yankee? George Bush? Tom Cruise?'

'No,' said Tim. 'I'm British.'

'Speak English?'

'Of course I do. I'm from England.'

'Me speak good English. You want help?'

'I'm lost,' said Tim. 'Which way is the Copacabana Castle?'

'Hotel? Yes?' When Tim nodded, the boy grinned. He

57

had brownish, crooked teeth. He muttered something to his friend, then grabbed Tim's sleeve. 'This way.' He pointed down a narrow alleyway. 'Come, here.'

Tim looked down the alleyway. It was dark and gloomy. Deep shadows hid the walls. Tim didn't like the idea of walking down there, unable to see where he was going, or who might be waiting. He said, 'That doesn't look right.'

'Yes, yes. Copacabana Castle, this way. Come.' The boy nodded, and smiled.

'Really? You're sure?'

'Yes, yes,' said the boy.

Tim looked at Grk. This was one of those moments when it would have been useful to speak Dog and ask Grk's advice. Should he walk down that dark, gloomy alleyway? Or should he continue walking the streets on his own, lost and lonely, trying to find his own way back to the hotel?

The boy said, 'What is your name?'

'Tim. And this is Grk.'

Hearing his name, Grk looked up, and wagged his tail.

The boy smiled. 'Me, Zito. My name, Zito. Understand? You Tim. Me Zito.'

'Nice to meet you, Zito,' said Tim.

Zito pointed at the other boy. 'This man, he Júnior. You Tim. Me Zito. He Júnior. Understand?'

'Yes,' said Tim. 'I understand. Hello, Júnior.'

Júnior opened his mouth in a big grin, but didn't speak. Most of his teeth were missing. Eating must have been difficult. Perhaps he stuck to soup and the odd ice cream.

58

'Come, Tim,' said Zito. 'We go to Copacabana Castle. This way.' Zito took a couple of paces towards the dark alleyway and waited for Tim to follow.

Tim had the sense that he probably shouldn't go down there, into that darkness, but he didn't know what else to do. His parents had told him a million times not to trust strangers. But he wasn't going to trust these two boys; he was just going to follow them back to the hotel.

Anyway, what could they do to him? They were just two boys. They weren't any older or bigger or stronger than him. In fact, they were both a bit smaller than him. And Tim wasn't alone: he had Grk to help him.

Everything would be fine, Tim decided. If the boys tried to attack, he would fight one of them, and Grk would fight the other, and together they would wrestle both Brazilian boys to the ground.

Tim said, 'Okay, let's go.'

'Good,' said Zito. 'This way.'

Zito walked first. Tim and Grk went next. Júnior came last.

After a few paces, the darkness surrounded them.

The ground was muddy. There were strange smells in the air, which reminded Tim of visiting a farmyard.

They turned a corner, then another. The air seemed to get even darker. Somewhere, someone was shouting, and a dog barked. Tim felt a bit nervous. Perhaps I've been stupid, he thought. Maybe this was a mistake. He thought about turning round and running back the way that they had come. But Júnior was directly behind him, blocking the way. There was no escape.

Tim gripped Grk's lead tightly. Grk was sniffing the ground. He didn't seem frightened; he was just fascinated by all the unusual smells.

They turned another corner, and walked down a long alleyway.

Zito stopped. He glanced both ways. He seemed to be listening for something or looking out for someone.

Tim said, 'What is it?'

Zito didn't answer. He just continued looking and listening.

'I don't understand,' said Tim. 'Why have we stopped? Where are we? What's going on?'

Zito smiled, and lifted his T-shirt, exposing his bare, brown belly. Tucked into the waistband of his shorts, there was something which looked like the handle of a gun. Zito gripped it in his right hand and pulled it out.

Tim blinked. To his amazement, he realised that it was a gun. A revolver. He was too surprised to speak.

Zito held the revolver with his right hand and clicked the safety-catch with his left hand. The gun was now ready to fire.

Down on the ground, Grk growled softly and opened his mouth, exposing small, sharp teeth.

Zito lifted the gun, and pointed it at Tim's head. 'Give me your money,' said Zito. 'Or I kill you.'

Chapter 13

Tim stared down the dark hole of the barrel.

He thought of the bullet waiting at the other end. He imagined the chain reaction that would occur when Zito pulled the trigger. Metal thumping into metal. Exploding gunpowder. A bullet travelling faster than the speed of sound. Before Tim even heard the noise of the explosion, the bullet would have left the gun, travelled the short distance between the barrel and his forehead, and killed him.

I'm staring at my own death, thought Tim.

Zito said, 'Now, you give me your money.'

'I don't have any money,' replied Tim.

Zito laughed. 'You are tourist. You stay in Copacabana Castle. Best hotel in Rio. You have money.'

'No, I don't,' said Tim.

Zito wrapped two fingers around the trigger, and smiled. 'You choose. Give me money. Or I kill you and take money. Which you want?'

'Neither,' said Tim. 'I might be staying in a posh hotel, but I didn't pay for it. The police are paying for me. Have you heard of Chief Careca? He's paying for me.'

Zito shook his head, looking disgusted. 'Liar.'

'I'm not lying,' said Tim.

'Liar,' repeated Zito. He muttered something in

Portuguese to Júnior, who giggled and said something in reply. They bantered back and forth, laughing and joking. Both of them seemed to have forgotten Tim, who couldn't understand a word that they said.

Taking advantage of their distraction, Grk jumped forward, his teeth bared, and bit Zito's ankle.

Zito screamed. He twisted round, throwing his foot around, trying to shake off Grk.

Tim sprang for the gun. He grabbed Zito's right hand with both of his. All three of them struggled desperately. Grk's teeth were wrapped around Zito's ankle. Tim and Zito grappled, each trying to get control of the gun.

Júnior ran across the alleyway, and jumped onto Tim's back. The four of them grunted and shouted. They fell over, and rolled across the ground, and struggled in a heap.

As suddenly as the fight had started, it ended. Júnior held one of Tim's arms. Zito held the other. Tim knew that trying to resist was pointless. Together, the two of them were too strong for him. Tim cried out, surrendering, and let his body go limp. He whistled to Grk. 'Let go,' he said in a low voice. 'Let go.'

Grk looked at Tim, surprised. He saw that Tim was serious. So he opened his mouth and released Zito's ankle.

Zito rolled away, rubbing his ankle with both hands. Then he stood up, and pointed the gun at Tim's head, and spoke to Júnior in Portuguese.

Júnior knelt beside Tim. He searched through Tim's pockets. He found nothing.

'Like I told you,' said Tim. 'I don't have any money.'

Júnior said something in Portuguese. Zito replied. They argued for a minute or two. Tim watched and waited. Eventually, Zito and Júnior seemed to reach some kind of agreement. Zito turned to Tim, and said, 'Okay. Get up. You come with us.'

'Where?'

'Maybe you don't have money. But your father do. We make kidnap. Come. This way.'

Tim had no choice. He pulled himself to his feet. He grabbed Grk's lead. Grk and Tim looked at one another. Neither of them said anything, but a kind of unspoken agreement seemed to pass between them. They would do as Zito said. They would be obedient. But both of them would wait for the right moment. And when that moment came, they would fight back.

The four of them walked down the alleyway. Júnior led the way. Tim came next, leading Grk on the lead. Zito followed. Every now and then, Zito pushed the barrel of the gun into Tim's back, reminding him not to run away or fight.

They walked through the favela. No one spoke.

The slums of Rio de Janeiro are called 'favelas'. They are cities within the city.

The poorest of the poor live in the favelas. Many of the residents are families who have come to the city from the countryside, searching for work. They can't afford proper houses. So they build a house for themselves, using whatever materials they can get for

63

little or no money. They use old bricks for the walls and a sheet of corrugated iron for the roof. Perhaps they have some clear plastic covering the window or perhaps they don't have any windows at all. Together, the whole family lives in one or two rooms.

Usually, houses inside the favelas have no electricity, no telephone lines and no clean water. The police rarely dare to venture inside the favelas, so the residents are just left to fend for themselves. Life is very difficult.

Tim glimpsed through big open windows into ramshackle houses. He saw children in rags standing in the street. There was a smell of dirt and heat.

Tim wondered where they were going. Once or twice, he was tempted to try running away, but he knew what would happen if he did. He would run down an alleyway, then another, and get lost. Zito and Júnior had probably been living in these streets for years, and perhaps for their entire lives, whereas Tim had never been here before. They would find him immediately. When they found him, Tim was certain, they would kick him or beat him or perhaps even shoot him.

So he didn't run away. What he did instead was this: he tried to remember exactly where they were walking. He stared at the streets and the buildings, memorising what he saw.

At some point, he would get an opportunity to escape. Zito and Júnior couldn't guard him all the time. They would have to sleep and eat and go to the loo. When that happened, Tim would run along this route and get back to where he had started.

They walked through a labyrinth of dark alleys and dirty streets.

Overhead, big, black birds soared through the sky. They were vultures. They searched the ground with their sharp eyes, looking for food. If they saw a scrap of meat, or an egg, or a wounded bird, or a dead rat, they would swoop down and start eating.

Just like everyone else in the favela, the vultures were hungry and desperate.

Grk stopped beside the entrance to an alleyway. His ears lifted. He growled softly.

'Hush,' said Tim.

Until that moment, Grk had behaved perfectly. He hadn't made a fuss. He hadn't tried to run away. He never growled or barked at any of the strange-looking people that they saw – and they had seen some people who looked very strange indeed.

They saw a fat man with a dead sheep slung around his shoulders.

They saw two thin young men running through the streets, carrying a rocket launcher and a box of grenades.

They saw a crazy man with foam dribbling from his lips, who stormed up and down the middle of the road, waving his arms, shouting and cursing at the top of his voice.

Grk hadn't growled or barked at any of them. He had just stared with an expression of fascination and curiosity.

But now, for the first time since they had walked into the favela, Grk growled.

He could smell something in the air. A very particular scent. It roused a memory, deep in his mind. Grk bared his teeth and made a low, furious growl, warning the owner of that scent that they would be well advised to keep a large distance between themselves and this particular dog.

Grk glanced at Tim, puzzled. Couldn't Tim smell it? Didn't he recognise this scent? Apparently not. Grk gave up on Tim and stared into the shadows again. His ears were upright and his hair stood on end. He growled again, louder.

Although Tim couldn't smell anything, he did know what that growl probably meant: Grk had seen something exciting. A squirrel, perhaps. Or a rabbit. Or a rat. Or a cat. Or even a chicken. He had seen something worth chasing.

'Not now,' whispered Tim. 'You can't chase anything now.' He pulled Grk's lead.

Júnior and Zito were impatient. They wanted to keep walking. Zito pushed Tim, and hissed, 'No stopping. No standing. Keep moving.'

Tim wanted to keep moving – but Grk wouldn't let him. Grk refused to budge. Tim tugged the lead, but he couldn't pull Grk away from the entrance to the alley.

Grk growled again. A long, loud growl.

Júnior and Zito stared at him, surprised and a little nervous. They hadn't expected such a small dog to sound so vicious.

Tim peered into the darkness, trying to see what might have interested Grk so much.

At that moment, the two Brazilian boys lost patience. Júnior clapped his hands. 'Move,' Zito said curtly. 'Move! Move!' He lifted his hand and pushed Tim in the middle of the back.

Just before Tim stumbled forward, he caught a brief glimpse of the thing that Grk had seen. It wasn't a rat or a cat, a squirrel or a rabbit. Not even a chicken. It was a man. Just an ordinary man. He had been walking from one doorway to another, carrying a plastic bag. He was wearing jeans and a T-shirt and a pair of flip-flops. He had black hair. His face was turned away, so Tim couldn't see his features.

Tim saw the man for less than a second. He didn't have a chance to register anything more than one simple fact: there was something odd about the man. Something unusual. Something which triggered a memory deep down in Tim's mind. But he wasn't sure what it was.

Then they were walking again, Júnior in the front, Zito at the rear, and Tim and Grk imprisoned between them.

After a few paces, Grk had forgotten whatever he had seen. There were too many other interesting things to be sniffed and watched. His hair flattened, and his ears lay down against the side of his head, and he thrust his nose at the ground, and sniffed and snuffled and snorted.

But Tim couldn't forget what he had seen. As they paced quickly down the alley, he tried to work it out.

What had been so strange about that man? What was unusual about him? What had Grk noticed that Tim was unable to see?

They turned a corner, then another, and walked down a narrow, dark alley. A stream of brown water ran along the ground. Júnior stopped beside a wooden door. He pushed it. The door creaked on its hinges and swung slowly open.

Zito put both his hands on Tim's back and, with a quick shove, pushed him through the doorway. Tim stumbled forward into the darkness.

Chapter 14

Back in the Copacabana Castle, the Malts were panicking. It was close to midnight. They had last seen Tim in the middle of the afternoon – almost eight hours ago.

When Max and Natascha returned from their tour of the city, they found the Malts lying asleep on the balcony. But there was no sign of Tim. Grk was missing too.

Max and Natascha woke Mr and Mrs Malt, and asked where Tim and Grk had gone. Immediately, Mr and Mrs Malt started panicking.

Together, all four of them searched the suite, but Tim and Grk weren't hiding in any of the rooms.

They left the suite and went in different directions, hurrying through the hotel, calling Tim's name and whistling for Grk. They searched the restaurants, the bars, the gym, the sauna, the swimming pool and even the casino, but they couldn't find Tim or Grk. They stopped people and said, 'Have you seen a small boy? An English boy? And a little dog?' But no one had.

The Malts and the Raffifis returned to their suite, and rang the police. Immediately, police units all over the city were alerted. But no one had seen a twelve-year-old British boy accompanied by a small white dog.

Later that night, Chief Careca came to make a

personal apology to the Malts. He explained that the police were searching the entire city. They were interviewing people and putting up posters. He didn't understand how Tim had managed to get out of the hotel, but he apologised on behalf of the Copacabana Castle, the police force and the city of Rio, and promised the Malts that their son would not come to any harm.

'Saying sorry is all very well,' said Mrs Malt. 'But what are you actually going to do?'

'We are making every effort to find your son,' replied the Chief of Police.

'But what are you actually doing?'

'I promise you, Mrs Malt, we are making every possible effort to discover your son.'

'You've said that already.' Mrs Malt spoke in a low, angry voice. 'But you haven't answered my question. What are you actually doing? How are you actually going to find him?'

Rather than answering, Chief Careca wiped his forehead with his silk handkerchief. He was sweating. He thought of all the other jobs that he could be doing. He could be a greengrocer. Or a postman. If only he had taken a different route in life, he would now be working as a gardener or a blacksmith or a mechanic in a garage. He could have been a fisherman, bobbing across the sea, relaxing in the sunshine. Chief Careca loved the sea. He would have been so happy to spend every day in a boat, pulling fish out of the water, feeling the salt spray against his bald head. Why hadn't he become a fishermen? Why did he ever choose to become a policeman? He could almost hear the water slapping against the side of the boat and smell the salt on the air...

He was snapped out of his dreaming by the angry voice of Mrs Malt. 'Tim is twelve years old,' she said. 'Do you understand what that means?'

'Yes, yes, of course I understand.' Chief Careca rubbed his eyes. He couldn't hear the wind any longer or smell the sea. He could just feel a dull pain behind his eyes. He was getting a migraine.

Mrs Malt raised her voice even louder. 'What's going to happen to him in the streets of Rio? How will he survive?'

'We will find him,' said Chief Careca. He wondered whether one of the waiters would be able to find an aspirin. 'You don't have to worry, Mrs Malt. My best men are searching the streets right now.'

'Your best men?' Mrs Malt shook her head. 'You mean the ones who have been searching for the Pelotti brothers? If they can't even find three vicious bank robbers, how are they going to find my son?'

Fifteen minutes later, Mrs Malt was standing on the balcony of the Copacabana Castle. She had her head in her hands. She was crying.

Mr Malt stood beside her. He put his arms around her shoulders.

Through her sobs, Mrs Malt whispered, 'Are we ever going to see Tim again?'

'Of course we are,' said Mr Malt. 'I'm sure we'll see him tomorrow.'

Mrs Malt buried her face in her hands and continued crying. She didn't believe him. And perhaps he didn't believe himself either.

Chapter 15

Tim tried to sleep. He was cold and hungry and frightened, but he knew that sleeping was more important than anything else. Tomorrow, he would need all his strength. Tomorrow, he might have to fight or run – and he would have no strength for fighting and running if he didn't sleep tonight.

But he couldn't sleep. He could hear strange noises. His feet were cold. He felt frightened and lonely.

He opened his eyes. Through the darkness, he saw the outlines of the room's other three occupants. Nearby, Grk was lying on the floor, snoring gently. On the other side of the room, Zito was asleep under a blanket. Júnior was curled against the door, stopping anyone from coming in or going out.

Tim closed his eyes again. He started counting. One, two, three, four, five, six, seven ... He reached forty-six, then lost count, and started again. The second time, he reached eighty-three before losing count. But he didn't feel tired.

He thought through the events of the previous day. He tried to remember his two routes through the city. Firstly, he tried to remember where he had walked with Grk when they left the hotel and headed through Rio's most elegant streets, past the shops and restaurants and offices. Secondly, he recalled walking with Zito and

Júnior through the alleys of the favela. If he could remember exactly where he walked, then he would be able to escape back along the same route.

He remembered the man that Grk had seen – the man who had made Grk growl. Tim had glimpsed him for less than a second, but tried to recall exactly what he had seen.

Black hair. Flip-flops. A white T-shirt. Blue jeans. A plastic bag.

A man with black hair, wearing flip-flops, blue jeans and a white T-shirt, carrying a plastic bag. What could be more ordinary than that?

But there had been something else. Something strange. Something about the man which triggered a distant memory in the back of Tim's mind. What was it? What was he trying to remember?

He had seen something without knowing that he was seeing it. But what? And how? And why? As his brain whirled in circles, his memories disintegrated into a series of fragments, none of which made any sense, and he drifted slowly into a deep sleep.

Breakfast consisted of some mouldy bread, brown water and a banana.

Tim passed a little scrap of bread to Grk, who sniffed it, and looked at Tim. Grk's expression seemed to be saying: *You expect me to eat this?*

Grk nudged the bread with his nose, then stared at Tim, blinking sadly, as if hoping he might get something better. Now his expression seemed to saying: *You are joking, aren't you?*

Zito broke a banana into three pieces, and gave a third each to Tim, Júnior and himself. The flesh of the banana was blackened and bruised.

Zito passed round an old glass filled with brownish water. They took turns to drink.

After breakfast, Júnior and Zito talked for a long time in Portuguese. They seemed to be arguing about something, although Tim had no idea what. He couldn't understand a word that they said.

All kinds of thoughts went through Tim's mind. He tried to imagine how his parents would be feeling. He wondered if there was any way to get a message to them. Could he ring them? Was there a phone anywhere?

He wished he had a mobile phone. His parents refused to buy one for him. They said he was too young. They said it was too expensive. But if they had given him a phone, he would now be able to call them. Perhaps this would finally persuade them to give him one.

He looked around Zito's home. There wasn't a phone here. The hut had no electricity. The only light came from a couple of candles.

The one-room hut was built of crumbling old bricks. Overhead, the roof was a sheet of corrugated iron. A draught blew through gaps in the walls. There was a wooden door but no windows.

How could he possibly escape? Even if he managed to get past Zito and Júnior, and reach the door, and flee from the room, he would be completely lost, adrift in the middle of a strange place. He would run down the alleyways, round and round in circles, until someone took pity on him. Or, more likely, decided to kidnap him themselves.

Júnior opened the door. Bright sunlight flooded into the room. Júnior hurried outside and closed the door after him. For a few moments, his footsteps echoed outside, and then he was gone.

Tim, Zito and Grk sat inside the hut for a long time, not speaking. Grk lay on the floor, his eyes half-closed, sleeping quietly. Zito lay against the wall, wrapped in his blanket, staring at the ceiling.

Tim remembered the gun tucked into the waistband of Zito's shorts and decided that trying to escape probably wasn't a great idea.

He thought through the events of the previous day. If he had just stayed in the suite, he would be sitting on the balcony now with his parents and Max and Natascha. He would be drinking fresh orange juice rather than brown water and eating a croissant rather than mouldy bread. Rather than a blackened banana, he would be able to choose from a huge basket of papayas, pineapples, cumquats, mangos and all kinds of other fruits whose names he didn't know.

What would his parents be doing now? And how would they be feeling?

Tim knew the answers to those questions. They would be panicking. They would be desperate to help him. But there was nothing they could do, because no one could possibly know he was here.

If he was going to escape, he would have to do it alone.

Zito was the first to break the silence. He said, 'You like Brazil?'

Tim nodded. 'It's okay.'

'First time here? In Brazil?'

'Yes.'

'Where you from? London?'

'Yes.'

They sat in silence for a little longer.

Then Tim asked a question. 'Where are your parents? Your mother and father? Where do they live?'

'I have no mother or no father,' said Zito. 'They dead.'

'Oh,' said Tim. He felt shocked. He tried to imagine how that would feel. He saw his mother and father every day, and relied on them for everything. Most of the time, it was true, he found them pretty annoying. They stopped him doing what he wanted. They forced him to go to bed early, and wouldn't give him money to buy stuff, and sent him to school in the mornings when he'd rather stay at home. But how would it feel to have no father and mother? How would it feel never to have had a father at all? Tim looked at Zito and said, 'So where do you live?'

'Here.' Zito gestured at the hut.

Tim was surprised. He had assumed that Zito was simply using this hut as a hide-out. 'You sleep here every night?'

'Yes.'

'Where do you wash? Where do you go to the toilet?'

'I show you. Come, come, see.' Zito stood up. Then

he thought of something. 'Wait. You make promise. You promise – no running. No try to escape. Okay?'

Tim stared at Zito. Should he promise that? He was about to refuse, when he suddenly realised what to do. He put his right hand behind his back, crossed his fingers, and said, 'I promise I won't run away.'

'Good,' said Zito.

They smiled at one another. Tim felt a bit guilty – he knew that he would break his promise at the first possible opportunity – but he didn't feel very guilty. After all, Zito had kidnapped him. You shouldn't feel any guilt about lying to someone who has kidnapped you.

Tim got a guided tour of Zito's home. It didn't take long. They paced from one end of the hut to the other, a journey which occupied no more than three or four steps.

In one corner, a sheet of cardboard lay on the floor, covered with an old blanket. That was Zito's bed.

At the back of the room, there was a tin of chickpeas and a tin of sardines on the floor. There was also an orange and a single slice of white bread covered in blobs of green mould. That was Zito's larder.

Tim and Zito walked outside, followed by Grk. The bright sunlight dazzled their eyes. Overhead, big black birds were flying in the clear blue sky.

A dirty stream ran down the middle of the street. The water was brown. That was Zito's bathroom.

Tim and Zito stood side by side, and peed in the stream.

Chapter 16

Around midday, Júnior returned with half a loaf of bread, three tomatoes and some yellow cheese. Zito divided it in three.

'This looks as if it's been rescued from a rubbish bin,' said Tim, turning the bread over and over in his hands.

'It was,' said Zito. He explained that he and Júnior got most of their food from rubbish bins around the city. Neither of them had parents, or brothers or sisters, or any other family. They lived alone. They had no one to help them. When they managed to get a little money by begging or stealing, they bought some food for themselves. Otherwise, they searched through rubbish bins outside hotels and restaurants and supermarkets, picking out whatever food had been thrown away.

Tim shared his portion with Grk, who ate the cheese in one gulp and the bread in another. Grk was now so hungry that he didn't care what he ate.

In the afternoon, Júnior went out again, leaving Tim, Grk and Zito in the hut. The three of them sat in silence for some time.

Tim had a lot to think about. He wondered how his parents might be feeling. He thought about that man with black hair, and wondered what had been unusual about him. He tried to recall the route that he had walked through the city and the favela, hoping that he might have a chance to walk it again in reverse. He wondered how to escape from the hut, and how to get away from Zito.

Tim had read a couple of books about kidnaps, and seen several movies on TV where people were held against their will. He tried to remember their tactics. What did they do? How did they free themselves?

Mostly, as far as he could remember, they didn't do anything. They just sat and waited for the police to rescue them.

Well, that wasn't much use. The police would never find him here. If he was going to escape, he would have to use his own ingenuity.

In one of the movies, Tim remembered, a woman had been kidnapped by three men. She made friends with them. At the end of the movie, one was ordered by the others to kill her.

The man led the woman into the forest. He lifted his gun and pointed it at her head. But then he pushed her away and told her to run. Rather than killing her, he let her escape, because he felt sorry for her.

I should make friends with Zito, Tim realised.

But how could he do that? How do you make friends with someone?

Tim had never deliberately tried to make friends with anyone. He didn't have very many friends. The friends that he did have, he had made by accident. At school, he had made friends with other boys by letting them play on his Gameboy. Or discussing the best type of bicycle. Or giggling together when the maths teacher came into the classroom with her skirt tucked into the back of her knickers. Or sitting next to someone in class, seeing them day after day after day after day after day after day after day after day after day after day after day after day after day after day after day after day after day after day until the holidays, when it felt strange not to see them any more.

All his friendships had happened by accident. And some of his friends, he didn't even like much.

Without Gameboys to play on or bikes to discuss or maths teachers to laugh at, Tim couldn't imagine how you could possibly become friends with anyone.

In the evening, Júnior came back to the hut with a heavy plastic bag.

As he did almost every night, Júnior had spent several hours walking through the city, going to restaurants, sneaking into the kitchens, begging the cooks for food. Sometimes, they gave him leftovers. Sometimes, they shooed him away with a broom.

Tonight, he had been lucky. There was a big fashion show in Rio. People had flown in from Paris, London, Milan, Los Angeles and New York. After the show, all the designers and models went out to dinner together. A grand meal had been cooked for them, consisting of several courses. However, models have to stay thin, so none of them ate more than a little soup, a few lettuce leaves, the odd slice of cucumber and some fruit. They didn't touch their steaks, their fish, their chips or their puddings.

Júnior opened his plastic bag, and spread a fabulous meal on the floor. They ate like princes. To start, they had prawn cocktails and chicken liver paté and slices of spicy salami. Next, they had grilled fish and big hunks of steak and chunky chips. To finish, they had chocolate puddings and meringues and peaches and mangos and little sugary biscuits studded with almonds. There was so much food, even Grk couldn't finish every scrap.

When the three boys had finished eating, they lay on the floor, clutching their stomachs and groaning. Grk lay beside Tim, licked his paws, closed his eyes, and started snoring.

A few minutes later, all four were asleep.

In the middle of the night, Tim woke up and realised what he had seen while they were walking through the favela.

Perhaps it had come to him in a dream. Perhaps his memory had just been working slowly while he slept. Perhaps his brain worked best when he was asleep.

It didn't really matter *how* it had happened. He didn't know why he knew or how he knew. What mattered was this: he knew.

The man in the alleyway. The one who Grk had growled at. The man with black hair and flip-flops and blue jeans and a white T-shirt. The man who was carrying a plastic bag.

Tim knew what was different about him.

The man had been carrying his plastic bag with his right hand. There was nothing unusual about that.

82

Ninety per cent of the human beings on this planet are right-handed.

But this particular man didn't have any choice. He couldn't possibly have carried the bag in his left hand, because he didn't have a left hand.

He only had one arm.

Chapter 17

At nine o'clock that night, Chief Careca came to the suite in the Copacabana Castle and delivered some news to the Malts. 'I don't know if it is good news or bad news,' he said, sighing softly. 'Maybe good. Maybe bad. Maybe good and bad.'

'Just tell us the news,' said Mr Malt. 'We can decide whether it's good or bad.'

'Wait,' said Mrs Malt. She hurried across the room, and knocked on the doors of the children's bedrooms. She summoned Max and Natascha to the table. She didn't want to keep any secrets from them. They would all hear the news together.

Max, Natascha and the Malts sat at the table, and listened to Chief Careca, who explained what had happened.

An hour ago, someone had telephoned the main reception at the Copacabana Castle. He didn't give his name, but he sounded like a small boy. From his accent, it was almost certain that he had been born and raised in Rio. He explained that he had news of Timothy Malt.

He was put through immediately to the hotel manager. The conversation was recorded.

The small boy said that he had kidnapped Timothy Malt. He demanded a ransom of one million dollars. He explained that he would call again in one or two days to arrange payment of the money. Then he ended the call.

The police had listened to the tape again and again, hunting for clues. Experts had been summoned from the best laboratories in Rio. They separated the sound on the tape into different frequencies, searching for background noise. They analysed the speaker's accent. They combed through his words, hunting for hidden meanings.

Chief Careca explained what the police experts had managed to deduce. Tim had probably been kidnapped by a gang of sophisticated criminals. They knew exactly what they were doing. They were professional, experienced and extremely capable. They must possess complicated electronic equipment. Whoever telephoned the Copacabana Castle had brilliantly disguised his voice, making himself sound exactly like a small boy.

At this point, Max interrupted: 'Perhaps it really was a small boy.'

'I don't think so,' replied Chief Careca, shaking his head and smiling as if Max had said something rather silly. 'Can you really imagine that a gang of sophisticated criminals would allow a small boy to make telephone calls on their behalf? Would they really use a small boy to make their ransom demands? Is that likely?'

'I suppose not,' said Max.

'Unless you think Tim has been kidnapped by a gang of small boys?'

Max shook his head. 'No, I don't.'

Mrs Malt said, 'So, who do you think has kidnapped him?'

Chief Careca shrugged his shoulders. 'Well, it is difficult to say. What I can know is this. We are dealing with sophisticated criminals. They broke into this hotel and took Tim from the room. You and your husband were here, but you heard nothing. No screams. No struggle. No shouting for help. These criminals are cunning and clever. They know exactly what they are doing. And, most importantly, they chose to kidnap Timothy Malt.' Chief Careca leaned forward, and dropped his voice to a whisper. 'Do you know who else is staying in the Copacabana Castle right now?'

The Malts, Max and Natascha shook their heads.

In a low voice, Chief Careca rattled off a list of names.

If you heard those names, you would recognise every single one of them. They were people whose names are mentioned constantly in the pages of magazines and newspapers around the world.

Just about every guest in the Copacabana Castle was excessively rich, exceptionally famous or exceedingly important. Some were all three.

At the other end of the corridor from the Malts and the Raffifis, for instance, there were two American actors whose last three movies had, between them, won eleven Oscars. On the floor below, there was a person closely connected to the British Royal Family, guarded by seven soldiers from the SAS. In one of the rooms by the swimming pool, the President of Nigeria's daughter was sharing a room with the son of a Greek tycoon. If you kidnapped any one of these people, you could demand a ransom of fifty million dollars, and you would be quite likely to get it.

'Why did they choose Tim?' said Mrs Malt. 'If they could have taken a film star or a president's daughter, why did they take my son?'

'For one reason, and one reason only,' said Chief Careca. 'Because by kidnapping Timothy Malt, they have a chance to attack the children of Gabriel Raffifi.'

Max gasped. Natascha sighed. Mrs Malt's face went white. Mr Malt said, 'It's not possible.'

'I am sorry, but it is possible,' said Chief Careca. 'Your son has been kidnapped by the Pelotti gang.'

Chapter 18

On Tim's second day in the hut, Zito described how he came to be living there.

In the morning, Tim, Júnior and Zito ate breakfast together, chewing the remains of the previous night's meal. The steak still tasted great, but the potatoes had gone soggy, and the chocolate pudding had acquired a thin layer of green mould. Grk scoffed all the scraps.

After breakfast, Júnior went out to make a phone call. Zito didn't say who Júnior would be phoning, or why.

When Júnior had gone, Zito started quizzing Tim about London. He wanted to know where Tim lived, and what his parents did, and how much they earned. Tim had the sense that this information would be used against him in some way, so he tried to reveal as little as possible. He changed the subject by asking Zito a series of questions: where he had been born, and what his father's job had been, and why he was now living alone.

Zito was happy to talk about himself. He liked the sound of his own voice and he couldn't often find people who were willing to listen.

He had been born in the north-east of Brazil, the poorest part of the country. He had three sisters and a brother. Zito was the youngest child in the family.

Zito's father was a fisherman. One night, there was a terrible storm which destroyed all the boats in the harbour. None of the fishermen could afford insurance, so the storm left Zito's father with nothing. Without a boat and unable to afford a new boat, he could not work as a fisherman. So he left the village and travelled to the nearest town, searching for a different way to support his family.

A month later, a grubby envelope arrived, addressed to Zito's mother. It contained a short letter and a few banknotes.

In the letter, Zito's father explained that he had found a job, working in a warehouse. He had earned enough money for a bus ticket to Rio and a little spare to send home to his wife. That night, for the first time in many weeks, Zito's family ate well.

Three months after that, a second letter arrived. Zito's father had arrived in Rio, and found a job in the docks, carrying goods on and off the boats. This time, he did not send any money.

A year passed without another letter.

Another year passed, and another, and still they heard nothing.

When four years had gone by, Zito's mother gathered up her five children, gave each of them a bag to carry, and led them to the road. She persuaded a taxi driver to give them a lift towards the nearest town. There, they begged a lift on a truck that was heading south.

For a fortnight, they travelled across Brazil, hopping from one truck to another. They begged bread and water from drivers and travellers. Every night, they went to sleep hungry. 'Wait till we arrive in Rio,' said Zito's mother. 'Your father will have a big house, and a garden, and a fridge, and as much food as you can eat. You just wait. Why do you think he has been quiet for all these years? Why do you think he hasn't written a single letter to us? Because he's been working so hard, that's why.'

When they arrived in Rio, they went to the address from which Zito's father had sent his last letter, four years ago. He didn't live there any more. The current occupants directed Zito's mother to another address. From there, they were sent somewhere else. Each address was cheaper and smellier than the one before.

When they finally found Zito's father, they did not recognise him. He had a long beard and grey hair. His hands shook. Between sentences, he swigged strong alcohol from a bottle wrapped in a brown paper bag.

Zito's father lived in one small room which contained two beds and a little stove. He shared the room with another man. There was no room for Zito, his mother, his brother and his sisters. But they had nowhere else to go. So they all slept in that tiny room. The whole family, two adults and five children, huddled together in one bed.

They had been in Rio for a month when Zito's brother was knocked down by a lorry. Because they could not afford to pay for a hospital bed, he received no medical treatment. After three days and three nights, he died.

A few months later, Zito's father was dead too, poisoned by the cheap alcohol that he couldn't stop drinking.

Zito's mother died a year after that. Over the

following few months, Zito's sisters disappeared one by one, until Zito was alone in the city. He had nowhere to live. He had no friends, no family, no money. He was eight years old. He walked into the centre of Rio, sat down on the pavement and lifted his hand to passers-by, begging for coins.

Since then, Zito had been living on the streets, begging and stealing whatever and whenever he could.

There were days when he had gone without food. There were nights when he had slept outside without even a blanket to cover himself. Often, even if he managed to get a little money, someone would simply steal it from him.

'Until I got this,' said Zito. He pulled up his T-shirt, showing off the gun tucked into the waistband of his shorts.

Tim stared at the gun. He wondered whether to make a lunge for it. Would he have time to grab the gun from Zito's belt before Zito grabbed it himself? And if he did, what could he do with it? Would he dare to point it at Zito?

'Now I'm going to be rich,' said Zito. 'I'm going to buy myself a Mercedes. I'm going to eat ice cream every day. I won't need this any more.' He dropped his T-shirt, hiding the gun again.

The chance had gone. In a way, Tim felt relieved. If he was going to escape, he would have to use his intelligence and his cunning, not violence. He turned to Zito, and said, 'All right, then. Tell me. How are you going to make all this money?'

'From the kidnap,' said Zito.

'From kidnapping me?'

'Exactly.' Zito grinned. 'Your mummy and your daddy get Tim. And I get one million dollars.'

'My parents don't have a million dollars,' said Tim. 'In fact, they don't have much money at all.'

Zito just laughed.

Tim knew that there was no point explaining that, yes, his parents certainly were rich compared to Zito or Júnior or the other residents of the favela, but they weren't so rich that they could get their hands on a million dollars. Rather than arguing or trying to explain, Tim said, 'What if you could get more money than that? All the money you want. And without breaking the law. How would you like that?'

Zito looked suspicious. 'I like it. Of course I like it. But how is it possible?'

'Have you heard of Pelottinho? And the Pelotti brothers?'

'Yes,' said Zito. 'Everyone knows who is Pelottinho.'

'If you catch him, the police will pay a huge reward. More money than you could ever need. And you won't have to steal it. You won't have to worry about being caught.'

Zito shook his head. 'To catch Pelottinho – this is not possible.'

'Why not?'

'Because no one know where he is.'

'I do,' said Tim.

Zito stared at him in astonishment. 'You?'

'Yes,' said Tim. 'Me.'

'You know where he is?'

'Yes.'

'Okay. Where he is?'

'I'll tell you,' said Tim. 'If you'll help me put him in prison.'

Chapter 19

Tim didn't understand what was happening.

Zito and Júnior had been arguing for ten or fifteen minutes. They were shouting at the top of their voices and waving their arms and stamping their feet. Both of them had red faces.

Finally, Tim couldn't stand it any longer. He interrupted, shouting in order to be heard over them: 'What's going on? What are you arguing about?'

Zito and Júnior stared at him for a second. Then they turned back to one another and continued arguing.

'Hey!' shouted Tim. 'Hey! Hey!' He clapped his hands together and shouted even louder: 'Hey! Listen to me for a minute! HEY!' When the two Brazilian boys finally shut up, Tim said, 'What is going on? What on earth are you arguing about?'

'He scared,' said Zito, pointing at Júnior.

Júnior shook his head and spat out a few words in Portuguese which Tim couldn't understand.

Tim said, 'Scared of what?'

'Scared of Pelotti,' said Zito. 'He no come with. Because scared. Understand?'

'I think so,' said Tim. 'He doesn't want to come with us. He's scared of the Pelotti brothers.'

Zito nodded. 'Most Pelottinho.'

'Most of all, he's scared of Pelottinho?'

Zito nodded again.

Tim shrugged his shoulders. 'That's okay. He doesn't have to come with us if he doesn't want to. But he could do one thing for us.'

'One thing?' said Zito. 'What thing?'

'Take off his clothes,' said Tim.

Zito laughed, then translated what Tim had said into Portuguese.

Júnior frowned and said, '*Por que*?'

Tim knew what that meant. '*Por que*' is the Portuguese word for 'Why'. So he explained. 'You're wearing the clothes of a boy who lives on the streets. I'm wearing the clothes of a boy who lives in a house in London. As soon as anyone looks at me, they know I'm not a street kid. They know I'm a tourist. So let's swap clothes. Give me your clothes and you can have mine.'

When Zito had translated all this into Portuguese, Júnior shrugged his shoulders and agreed. Tim and Júnior stripped off their clothes. Júnior put on Tim's shirt, shoes, socks and trousers. Tim put on Júnior's T-shirt and shorts.

Júnior swaggered up and down the hut in Tim's clothes. He grinned happily.

Tim wasn't so cheerful. Júnior's T-shirt was covered in dirt and Júnior's shorts had a nasty smell, as if someone had been sick on them, quite a long time ago.

But Tim knew that he had no choice: there wasn't time to wash the clothes, so he just had to put up with the stink. Trying to breathe through his mouth rather than his nose, Tim pulled on the smelly shorts and the dirty T-shirt. He wiped some mud over his face and his legs, then ruffled his hair. If you had seen him, you would have assumed that he was just one of the homeless kids in the favela who spent their days begging for food and their nights sleeping on the streets. If you were generous, you might have given him a few coins or half your sandwich.

Once the streets were dark, Zito and Tim said goodbye to Júnior.

Júnior said something in Portuguese that Tim couldn't understand.

'He say, good luck,' translated Zito.

'*Obrigado*,' said Tim. That is the Portugese word for 'thank you'.

Zito, Tim and Grk hurried out of the hut, leaving Júnior behind. Júnior stood in the doorway for a moment, waving goodbye. Then he went back inside to continue admiring his new clothes.

As Zito and Tim walked through the favela, no one took any notice of them. They were just two small boys, slipping through the shadows, heading into the city to hunt for food.

Grk stopped every few paces to smell something interesting, then bounded after them, his tail wagging, his eyes bright and excited.

Zito led the way. He guided them back along the route that they had come. After they had been walking for five or ten minutes, Tim nodded and whispered, 'This is it. This is the place.'

It was a slim, dingy alley. Flies swarmed around piles of discarded rubbish. A dead rat lay on the ground. The air stank like a toilet that hasn't been flushed.

The alley had two entrances. Zito waited at one end. Tim and Grk waited at the other. No one could come or go without passing them.

Tim squatted on the floor, just as Zito had told him to do. He held out his right hand at anyone who passed, his palm open, begging for money. No one took any notice of him. Grk curled up at Tim's feet.

After a few minutes, Tim had a surprising thought.

I could just get up, he thought. And walk away.

No one would try to stop him.

I've been kidnapped, thought Tim. By a boy with a gun. And now he's gone away. The gun isn't pointing at me. I should escape. I should stand up and run down the street and get away as quickly as possible.

But if he did that, what would he say to Natascha and Max when he got back to the hotel? 'I found the Pelotti brothers,' he would say. 'And then I ran away. Because I was scared. Because I was tired and hungry. Because I wanted to be with my mum and dad.'

Tim shook his head. He wasn't going to do that. He was going to stay here, and catch the Pelottis, and deliver them to jail.

They sat there for a long time. Tim begged and Grk slept.

As a beggar, Tim had very little success. A couple of people did put some odds and ends into his open palm:

97

a stone and a piece of chewing-gum (still in the packet) and a box of matches and an orange. But not a single coin.

As the night went on, fewer and fewer people walked past. The favela grew quieter. Lights went out. Radios were switched off. Conversations came to an end. Silence descended. On the empty streets, nothing moved.

Tim was woken by a low, deep growl.

He opened his eyes.

For a second, he couldn't remember how he came to be here. What was he doing, sitting on the pavement? Why was he leaning against a crumbly old wall? Then he remembered and immediately cursed himself for falling asleep. What had he missed? Had Zito fallen asleep too? Had the Pelottis sneaked past them and escaped?

Grk was leaning forward. His ears stood upright. He was growling slowly and quietly. He sounded like an aeroplane preparing to take off.

'Sssshhh,' whispered Tim. He put his hand on Grk's back, and gently stroked his fur. 'Sssshhh.'

Grk understood immediately what he should do. He stopped growling, but continued peering down the alleyway.

Tim stared in the same direction. His eyes took some time to adjust. Dogs can see much more clearly in darkness than humans. After twenty or thirty seconds, Tim finally distinguished some shapes in the gloom. Three men had emerged from a doorway. They were talking to one another in low voices. It was impossible to hear what they were saying, or even what language they were using.

The three men started walking towards Tim.

Tim panicked. He didn't have time to run or hide. What could he do?

He did the only thing that he could possibly do in the circumstances. He sat perfectly still and pretended to be asleep.

Grk watched the three men as they came closer. They were walking slowly and casually. None of them spoke.

Tim half-closed his eyes. In the darkness, no one would know that he was awake. They would think that he was just a homeless boy, sleeping on the pavement because he had nowhere else to go.

When the three men reached Tim, they stopped. One of them pointed at Grk and said something in Portuguese. The other two men laughed.

Tim breathed slowly and calmly, letting the breath flow gradually in and out of his body.

One of the men leaned down and stroked the top of Grk's head.

The man had only one arm. It was Pelottinho. He tickled Grk's ears.

Grk just wanted to do one thing. Jump up and bury his teeth in Pelottinho's hand. But Grk knew that biting people is wrong. So he sat still and allowed himself to be tickled.

Pelottinho straightened up. The three men walked slowly down the alleyway.

Grk rolled over and over in the mud. He rubbed his head against the ground. He wanted to get rid of Pelottinho's scent, to smear it off his fur, to replace it with the smell of dirt instead.

When the three men reached the end of the alley and turned the corner, Tim whistled.

Immediately, he was answered by another whistle. A moment later, Zito came running. Tim sprang to his feet. They sprinted down the alley, pursuing the Pelotti brothers, followed by Grk.

The Pelotti brothers walked quickly and confidently through the narrow alleys of the favela. They never turned round. They never looked back. They never saw the three small shapes which darted behind them, hurrying from corner to corner.

They reached a main road. A black VW Golf was parked in the street. It had darkened windows. The Pelottis got inside.

Tim looked at Zito. 'What do we do now?'

'Follow them.'

'Yes, but how?'

Zito glanced around. He stared at the cars parked on both sides of the road. 'You ride bike? You know how?'

'A bicycle? Of course. Don't you?'

'Not bicycle. Motorbike. You ride motorbike?'

Tim shook his head. 'I'm only twelve. You have to be seventeen to ride a motorbike.'

'Not in Brazil. Come.' He hurried along the street, followed by Tim.

Twenty or thirty motorbikes and scooters were parked in a line. Zito hurried along the line, inspecting each of the bikes in turn. 'Some easy to steal,' he said. 'Some not easy. Ah! Yes! This one.' He darted forward. One of the motorbikes was older than the others. It didn't have a good modern lock. Zito took a knife from his pocket. He fiddled for a few seconds with the motorbike's ignition.

At the other end of the street, an engine roared. It was the VW Golf. The Pelotti brothers were ready to go. Their car eased away from the kerb.

'Quick,' hissed Tim. 'They're getting away.'

'Okay, okay. I do it.' Zito twisted the knife back and forth.

To his horror, Tim saw the Golf speeding down the road away from them. In a few seconds, it would turn the corner and disappear into the city. Then they would never find it again. He had been so close to the Pelottis – so close that he could have touched them – but in a few seconds, they would be gone for ever. 'Hurry, they're getting away,' he whispered. 'Please, be quick.'

Without answering, Zito leaned forward, concentrating on what he was trying to do. He pushed the knife harder. There was a sound like a twig snapping. 'All done,' said Zito. He twisted the throttle. The engine roared. Zito swung his leg over the seat and climbed onto the motorbike.

He was too small to touch the ground with his legs. He could only keep his balance by revving the engine and moving slowly forward.

'HEY, TIM!' Zito shouted at the top of his voice to be heard over the engine. 'WE GO! COME! COME!'

Tim jumped on to the back of the motorbike and wrapped his arms around Zito's middle. The bike wobbled. Grk squirmed between them, tucking himself in the tight space between Tim's chest and Zito's back. Zito yelled, 'HOLD ON! KEEP TIGHT!' He revved the engine. The motorbike lurched forward. They roared down the street and skidded round the corner.

They hadn't lost the Pelottis. The VW Golf was ahead of them. Zito was careful not to get too close, because he didn't want the Pelottis to realise that they were being followed.

The streets of Rio were full of people and cars. Cariocas love to stay up late, eating and drinking and dancing. (As you probably know, people who live in Rio are called Cariocas.) If the streets had been completely empty, perhaps the Pelottis would have realised that they were being followed by two boys and a dog on a motorbike. But Zito could hide behind other cars, and follow the black Golf without being spotted.

They drove down the hill, through the centre of Rio and onto the highway. The Golf accelerated. So did Zito. The motorbike wobbled from side to side. The wind battered them, tearing at their clothes and hair, slapping their faces.

I'm not wearing a helmet, thought Tim. If I fall off, I'm dead.

Simple as that. I'm dead.

A thought flashed through his mind: this is the most terrifying thing that has ever happened to me.

He closed his eyes and waited for it to end.

Then he realised something quite surprising. Although it was quite possible that he would die very soon, he was enjoying himself. He opened his eyes and stared at the Golf, two or three hundred yards ahead on the highway. Then he turned his head and watched the landscape flashing past at great speed. He couldn't help it: he grinned. A big, happy smile spread across his face.

Riding on the back of the bike was the most frightening thing that had ever happened to him – but it was also one of the most thrilling. Perhaps excitement and fear are the same thing. Perhaps you can't be excited without being frightened too.

Soon the wind was blowing so hard that all Tim's thoughts were blown out of his skull. He just opened his eyes and enjoyed the ride. At great speed, they zoomed along the highway. The sea was on their right and the city was on their left. Streaks of light appeared in the sky. The night was ending. Dawn was coming.

The Golf turned off the highway and drove down a slip-road. A couple of hundred yards behind, the motorbike followed. They drove round three roundabouts and alongside the high metal fence that prevented intruders from entering the airport.

A red metal barrier blocked the road. As the Golf approached, Pablo Pelotti pressed a remote control inside the car, and the barrier lifted automatically.

The Golf drove under the barrier and sped across the tarmac, heading for a group of aircraft hangars with grey walls and green roofs.

Zito accelerated to follow the Golf.

Too late, Zito realised his mistake. The barrier was closing – and he didn't have a remote control to make it open again.

He grabbed the motorbike's brakes. But it was no good. He couldn't stop in time. The front wheel thumped into the barrier and twisted sharply to the left. With a loud BANG, the barrier splintered into pieces and the bike skidded across the ground. Grk went flying. The two boys rolled over and over. Zito screamed. Tim smacked his head against a metal post, and everything went black.

Chapter 20

'Wake up! Hey! Wake up!'

'I'm not going to school,' mumbled Tim. 'I've got a headache.'

'Come on! We must move!'

'Stop shaking me. I'm sick.'

'Wake up! You idiot!'

'Don't call me an idiot,' said Tim, and opened his eyes. To his amazement, he discovered that he wasn't in bed, and the hands shaking him awake didn't belong to his mum. No – he was lying on a patch of cold tarmac and a small dirty boy was leaning over him, demanding that he get up.

Immediately, Tim remembered where he was and what had happened. He struggled to his feet.

Nearby, Grk was sprawled on the tarmac, licking his paws. A little further away, the motorbike was lying in a heap, smashed to pieces. Shards of metal lay all around. A pool of dark liquid was spilling from the fuel tank and spreading slowly across the tarmac.

Tim looked around. On the other side of the airfield, a few men in overalls were working with pipes and tankers. Several green trucks were driving slowly alongside the perimeter fence. But there was no sign of the black VW Golf. Tim looked at Zito. 'Where are the Pelottis?'

'There.' Zito pointed towards the row of aircraft hangars. 'They go inside.'

'Did you see which one?'

'Yes. Number three. Green door.'

Tim nodded. Without another word, he started running across the tarmac towards the hangar with the green door. Grk followed immediately. Zito hesitated for a second, then followed too.

The sky was beginning to get light. Soon, the sun would rise. Huge passenger planes were circling overhead, preparing to land on the runway. Throughout the day, another passenger plane would land every two or three minutes, bringing people from all around the world to Rio.

When the three of them reached the edge of the hangar, Tim signalled to Zito, telling him to wait. Zito said, 'Why? I want come too.'

'Shh!' Tim put his finger to his lips.

'Sorry,' whispered Zito. 'But why I wait? I want come too.'

'If I don't come back in five minutes, you fetch the police. Okay? You understand?'

Zito looked worried. He was about to say something, then he thought better of it, and just nodded.

'Good,' whispered Tim. 'Wait here.' He looked down at Grk. 'Grk – you wait too. Okay? Wait!'

Grk wagged his tail. Maybe he understood and maybe he didn't. It was impossible to tell. But when Tim started walking away, Grk waited with Zito, just as he had been instructed.

106

Alone, Tim crept along the length of the hangar, keeping low, taking care not to be seen. He looked from left to right, but he couldn't see the Pelottis or their VW Golf. He eased slowly further forward until he reached the edge of the huge metal door. He waited there for a few seconds, listening for voices or footsteps. He couldn't hear anything. He stuck his head round the corner of the door and peered into the hangar.

Inside, he could see the black Golf and a small silver jet plane, parked side by side. The plane was the type that rich businessmen use to fly from one city to another. A man in a black uniform was walking down the metal staircase that led into the cabin. When he reached the tarmac, he continued briskly to the back of the hangar, and went through a door. There was no sign of anyone else.

Tim wondered what to do. Should he run to the main airport buildings and find the police immediately? But what if it was all a mistake? What if they had followed the wrong VW Golf? What if this plane actually belonged to an innocent businessman? What if the Pelottis were in another hangar, somewhere else in the airport, climbing aboard a completely different plane, preparing to fly away?

Before doing anything else, Tim realised, he would have to check that the Pelottis were actually here. Once he had seen them for himself, he would fetch the police.

Tim turned round. Twenty feet away, Zito and Grk were squatting on the ground, waiting and watching. Tim held up his hand, telling them to stay exactly where they were. Then he shuffled forwards, moving round the corner, and tiptoed into the hangar.

He moved very slowly. Before taking a step, he waited, looking and listening, searching for any sign of the Pelotti brothers. He couldn't see or hear anyone. Perhaps they were inside the plane. Or perhaps they were somewhere else entirely.

The huge hangar was filled with boxes, crates and cabinets. Tools lay on the floor. Three hefty cables were fixed to the plane.

Tim could see through the windows into the plane. The lights were on, but there didn't seem to be anyone inside.

He strode up the first two metal stairs and peered through the window. He could see several plush seats, covered in black leather, and a pile of brown sacks, filling the back of the cabin.

Those sacks must contain all the money that the Pelottis had stolen during their bank robberies. So this was their plane.

Tim knew what he should do. He should turn round, walk down the steps and find a phone. He should ring the police. This was their work, not his.

But something drew him towards the plane.

He climbed the last couple of stairs, and walked inside.

Chapter 21

The plane was small but luxurious. It was divided into three sections. At the front, there was a cockpit for the pilot and the co-pilot. A door separated them from the passengers. The second section, the main body of the plane, had four big plush leather armchairs and a wooden table. A big TV screen hung from the ceiling. It looked more like a posh hotel room than the inside of an aeroplane. The third section, at the back of the plane, had a toilet and a small kitchen.

A pile of large brown sacks filled the back of the plane.

Tim pressed his hands against one of the sacks. It felt squashy. Like a beanbag. He felt another sack, and another. They felt just the same.

He had a pretty good idea what was inside the sacks, but he wanted to be sure. Each one was fastened with a length of blue string, tied in a taut knot. Tim reached for the nearest sack and untied the string. He pulled the sack open and looked inside.

Most beanbags contain beans. These ones were filled with paper.

Tim took a step backwards. There were thirty or forty sacks. Each was stuffed with cash. This was the loot that the Pelottis had stolen from the banks of Rio.

With the contents of these forty sacks, you could live

happily for the rest of your life. You could spend every day doing whatever you wanted. Playing computer games. Eating pizza and ice cream. Watching movies. Sailing across the oceans in a huge yacht. Never working. Never taking orders from anyone. Never having to worry about anything.

If I kept it, thought Tim, who would know? Who would care?

Maybe I should go to the front of the plane, he thought, and start the engine and fly away from here.

Flying a plane couldn't be that difficult. You just press the button to start the engine, then move the lever to make the plane whizz along the runway and shoot into the air.

He could fly out of Rio and head across the sea.

He would land in an airport far away from here. No one would know who he was. He would buy a huge house. He would hire fifty servants. He would do exactly as he pleased.

Every morning, he would lie in bed as long as he wanted. Every afternoon, he would go to the garage where he kept his collection of sports cars. He would pick a different Porsche or Ferrari or Lamborghini, and spend several hours driving round and round his own private race track. Every evening, he would watch kung fu movies in his private cinema and eat nothing but chocolate ice cream.

He would be the happiest man on earth.

There were only three problems. Problem number one: he wasn't completely sure that he really knew how to fly

110

a jet. Problem number two: he would always be worried that the police were going to come and catch him. Problem number three: the money didn't belong to him.

Of these three problems, the third seemed the most difficult.

Tim didn't like the idea of stealing other people's money.

He thought about all the people that he had seen in Rio. The businessmen in the street. The shopkeepers selling pineapples and papayas and watermelons. The one-legged beggars slumped on the pavement, holding out their palms to passers-by. The money belonged to them, not to him.

Tim knew what he should do: he should deliver this plane and its contents to the police. They would pay him a reward. It wouldn't make him the richest man in the world. He wouldn't be able to afford a private cinema or a Lamborghini. But the reward would probably be big enough to buy a new TV, some new games for his computer and a few tubs of chocolate ice cream. He would have to be satisfied with that.

Tim turned round. There was a man standing in the doorway.

No, not a man. A boy.

A boy and a dog.

Tim said, 'What are you doing here? I told you to wait for me.'

Grk wagged his tail and yelped happily. He was delighted to see Tim.

Zito didn't seem to hear Tim's question or even see

Tim. His eyes were big and wide. He stared at the money pouring out of the sack that Tim had opened and all the other sacks piled up at the back of the plane. He whispered something in Portuguese.

'Get out,' said Tim. 'Go back.'

Zito shook his head slowly from side to side. 'We be rich,' he whispered.

'Come on, get out. We have to get the police before the Pelottis come back.'

Zito didn't seem to hear what Tim was saying. He padded across the carpet and plunged his hands into the open sack. With both hands, he lifted up a pile of cash. 'Look at this,' he whispered. 'We be rich!'

'That money doesn't belong to us,' said Tim. 'It belongs to the people who put it in the bank. We have to give it back to them.'

'Why?'

'Because it's theirs.'

'They will never know.' Zito grabbed a handful of notes and stuffed them in his pocket. 'Come on,' he said. 'Take! Take! Quick!'

Tim shook his head. 'I'm getting the police.'

'No!' Zito turned round, his eyes flashing with fury. 'This money for us!'

'The police will pay a reward for catching the Pelottis. You'll have to be satisfied with that.'

'Reward?' Zito laughed. 'What could be more good reward than this?' With a beaming smile, Zito stared at the stacks of banknotes. He rubbed his hands together. 'Okay, what now? How we get out?'

'It's not ours,' said Tim. 'We can't keep it.'

'If you no want, I keep all.'

'Neither of us are going to keep it,' said Tim. 'We're going to give it back to the people who own it.'

The smile vanished from Zito's face. He shook his head, then jabbed his forefinger at Tim. 'You... You have easy life. Father. Mother. House. Dog. You have everything. So you don't need no money. Me – I have nothing. Understand?'

Tim nodded. 'Of course I understand.'

'No, no. You no understand.' Zito scooped a handful of money from the sack, then let the notes slither through his fingers. 'This money – this change my life. Okay? With this, I start live. No more sleep in street. No more eat from rubbish. With this, I live. You understand?'

Tim thought for a moment. Then he said, 'I'm sure the police will help you. They'll be so grateful that we've found the Pelottis, they'll do whatever they can for you.'

'Police? They don't do nothing. Police is liars.' Spitting out those words, Zito plunged both his hands into the open sack, pulled out a hunk of banknotes and stuffed them into the pockets of his shorts.

'Don't do that,' said Tim.

Zito took no notice. He continued filling his pockets. Banknotes spilled onto the floor, forming a pool of money around his feet, but he didn't bother reaching down to pick them up. When his pockets were full, he grabbed more banknotes and pushed them inside his

113

T-shirt. He grabbed his pistol, which was tucked in the waistband of his shorts, and tossed it on the floor. With all this money, he could buy twenty more pistols. Or a bazooka. Even a tank. He filled his shorts with money.

'I'm going now,' said Tim. 'You can come with me or you can stay here. It's up to you.'

Zito ignored him, and continued stuffing money into his shorts and T-shirt. His belly had swelled to twice its usual size.

''Bye, then,' said Tim.

'Ciao,' said Zito, not even turning to look at Tim.

Tim walked towards the door. He no longer cared what Zito did. He was determined to fetch the police and let them deal with all this.

Just as Tim reached the door of the plane, he froze.

There was a sound from outside. Footsteps on the tarmac. Voices. People were walking through the hangar.

Tim and Zito stared at one another, both of them suddenly terrified.

The footsteps came closer. There was the clang of metal. Whoever they were, they had started climbing the steps that led into the plane.

Grk's hair stood on end. He sniffed the air. He could smell someone bad. He didn't know who it was; he just knew that he didn't like their smell. He started growling – a low, angry growl.

'Sshh,' hissed Tim. He looked around, searching for somewhere to hide. Behind the armchairs? In the cockpit? Or the toilet? Then he spotted a possible place.

He reached down and grabbed Grk in his arms. 'In here,' he whispered to Zito. 'Quick!' Tim ducked behind the sacks, carrying Grk, and squatted on the ground.

Zito stood still. He didn't know what to do. He had banknotes in both hands, and more stuffed up his T-shirt and in his pockets. He didn't have time to get rid of them. Holding the money, he jumped after Tim, and wriggled behind the sacks.

Tim and Zito looked at one another. Neither of them dared speak. They crouched behind the sacks, trying not to make a sound.

Their view was blocked by the sacks. They couldn't see anything; they could only hear what was happening. They heard footsteps and voices. Metal banged against metal. People talked in Portuguese. All the voices belonged to men. Tim couldn't understand a word that they said.

Zito's eyes widened. He remembered his gun. He'd dropped it on the floor. Not only was he now defenceless, but one of the men might notice a pistol lying on the floor and wonder what had happened to its owner. They might start searching the plane. If they did, Zito and Tim would have no way to protect themselves.

Tim peered through a gap between the sacks. He saw four men. Three of them were sitting on the leather armchairs. They were the three Pelotti brothers.

The fourth man was standing in the doorway. He was wearing a black uniform and a black cap with golden tassels. Tim guessed that he must be the pilot. One of the

115

Pelottis seemed to be telling him what to do. The pilot listened to his instructions, then nodded, ducked under the low doorway and settled himself in a chair in the cockpit. Without any hesitation, he started fiddling with the switches, preparing for take-off.

The three Pelotti brothers lounged on the leather chairs. Tim stared at them. He was only a few feet away. He could have stretched forward and touched them.

The engines roared. The plane shuddered, then eased forward.

Tim slid back and took his place beside Zito and Grk.

The plane taxied across the runway. Sitting in the back, hidden beside the sacks, Tim and Zito couldn't see through the windows. They had no idea where they were going. All they could do was wait and see what happened.

After waiting a few minutes for instructions from the control tower, the pilot steered the plane onto the runway, then accelerated. The engines boomed. The plane raced along the tarmac, faster and faster, and shot into the air.

Grk rolled across the floor.

His paws scrabbled desperately, but he couldn't get any grip on the smooth surface.

Tim and Zito didn't see him. They were pinned against the back wall, trying to cling to the walls. They didn't want to be jolted forwards. If that happened, they might roll down the plane and land at the feet of the Pelotti brothers.

Grk yelped desperately, crying out for help, trying to

get Tim and Zito's attention. But they couldn't hear him, because the engines were too loud.

The plane tipped over to the right, and circled over the city.

Grk whizzed backwards. He rolled across the floor. His paws waved in the air. He smacked into the door of the toilet.

The door swung open. Grk slid into the toilet.

The plane tipped to the left and headed for the mountains.

The door of the toilet slammed shut, locking Grk inside.

In the cockpit, the pilot spoke over the radio to the control tower. He described the route that he intended to take. The control tower issued him with a flight path. The pilot pointed the plane towards the west.

As far as anyone in the control tower knew, the plane was just carrying a group of rich businessmen to a meeting in Brasilia, the capital of Brazil.

Chapter 22

Chief Careca had called every member of the police force back from holiday. He recalled old men who had retired from the police force years ago. He insisted that sick officers leave their beds. He summoned the traffic wardens and the museum guards and the immigration officers. He ordered the filing-clerks to stop filing and the computer technicians to abandon their computers. Even the chefs who worked in the police canteens were pulled out of their kitchens and put on active duty.

'Find the Pelottis,' said Chief Careca. 'Find Timothy Malt!'

Twenty thousand policemen and policewomen paced the pavements of Rio. They checked identity cards and peered through windows and knocked on doors. They were searching for the three Pelotti brothers, a boy called Tim and a dog called Grk.

None of them looked up at the sky. None of them noticed a small plane disappearing into the clouds. None of them realised that Tim, Grk and the three Pelotti brothers had already left the city.

118

Chapter 23

The plane flew towards Brasilia for an hour, then changed direction and headed for the jungle.

Tim and Zito had no idea where the plane was actually going, nor where it was supposedly going. For now, they just cared about one thing: they didn't want to be found by the Pelottis. They crouched behind the pile of sacks, not talking, breathing quietly, trying not to make any noise.

Through a gap in the sacks, Tim could see the three Pelotti brothers, relaxing in the cabin.

Pelotinnho lay on the long leather sofa and drifted into a deep sleep.

José Pelotti picked up the remote control and switched on the TV, flicking through the channels till he found a football match.

Pablo Pelotti sat in one of the armchairs and read *Learn English in One Month*. Pablo had been reading the book for two years and he was still on the second chapter. He recited the words quietly to himself. 'I am,' he whispered. 'You are. He is, she is, it is. We are. You are. They are.'

Pablo closed the book and tried to remember what he had just read. 'I am,' he whispered. He paused for a moment, trying to remember what came next. Then he whispered: 'You am. He am. She am. It am. We am. You

119

am. They am.' He shook his head, knowing that he had got it wrong, and opened the book again.

For an hour or two, nothing else happened. Pelottinho slept, José watched TV and Pablo tried to learn English.

Zito fell asleep too. His head nodded forward and he drifted into a shallow doze.

Tim couldn't understand how anyone could sleep at a time like this. He was too worried to sleep. A thousand thoughts whirled in his head. He thought about his parents. He worried about Max and Natascha. He tried to imagine where the plane might be headed. He wondered what on earth had happened to Grk.

As soon as the flight started, Tim realised that Grk had disappeared. He looked around. He shuffled forwards and peered through a gap between the sacks. There seemed to be no sign of Grk.

Where could he be?

He must be hiding under one of the armchairs, Tim decided. Or perhaps he had run into the cockpit and sheltered under the pilot's chair.

Grk was a sensible dog. He would know what to do. He would keep himself hidden and wait until they arrived at their destination.

That's what Tim did too. While Zito slept, Tim settled down behind the sacks and waited to see what would happen next.

Pelottinho woke up and yawned. He rubbed his eyes. He stretched his arm. He stood up and walked towards the sacks of money.

Tim sat absolutely still. What if Pelottinho came to look at the cash? What if he pulled the sacks aside? There was nowhere for Tim to run. And he couldn't fight. So what could he do?

Beside him, Zito was still sleeping silently. Please don't snore, thought Tim. Whatever you do, don't snore.

Pelottinho eased himself round the sacks. He walked to the toilet. He opened the door, went inside, and shut the door again. There was a loud CLICKITY-CLUNK as Pelottinho locked himself inside the toilet.

The noise woke Zito. He sat up, blinking, and looked around. Then he gazed at Tim. 'What happens?'

Tim put his finger to his lips. 'Sssshh.'

Zito nodded. In a very quiet voice, he whispered, 'What happens?'

'Nothing,' whispered Tim. 'We are still flying. I don't know where we're going.'

Zito nodded again. He looked around. 'Where the dog?'

'I don't know,' said Tim.

Zito nodded for a third time.

At that moment, a loud roaring noise came from the toilet. It sounded something like this: 'WHHOOOAAAAAAAAHHHH!!!!'

José Pelotti dropped the remote control and jumped to his feet. Pablo Pelotti threw his book on the floor and jumped to his feet too.

Tim and Zito spun round to see what had happened.

With a CLUNKETY-CLICK, the door opened.

Pelottinho ran out of the toilet with his trousers round his ankles. He had a wild expression in his face. His eyes were wide. His hair was standing on end. He ran the length of the plane until he reached his two brothers. Then he shouted at the top of his voice: '*Fui mordido no bum-bum por um monstro branco!*'

If you can read Portuguese, you'll understand exactly what he meant.

If you can't, you won't. So I'll translate it for you. This is what Pelottinho shouted: 'I've been bitten on the bum by a white monster!'

Chapter 24

Pablo Pelotti was the oldest of the three Pelotti brothers, and the most sensible, and so he always took charge when things went wrong.

When the Pelottis were little children, their parents died, so they had to look after themselves. Pablo was the one who organised which of the brothers laid the table, which of them cooked the dinner and which of them washed the dishes.

When the Pelottis were just three young crooks, starting out on their criminal career, Pablo was the one who made all the decisions. On the afternoon that they first stole some cakes from the bakery, Pablo organised a distraction so the baker would be looking in the wrong direction. When they first grabbed a handbag from a woman in the street, Pablo decided which of the brothers would bump into her, which of them would pull the bag from her shoulder and which of them would make his escape on a moped. When the Pelottis robbed their first bank, Pablo decided who stood by the door, who pointed a gun at the customers and who went into the vault with the manager.

So when Pelottinho came out of the toilet, screaming that he had been bitten on the bum by a white monster, Pablo took control of the situation. Before doing anything else, he ordered Pelottinho to pull up his

123

trousers, zip his zip and tie his belt. Pelottinho did as he was told. Then, Pablo eased past the big pile of sacks, walked to the back of the plane and had a look in the toilet.

He saw a dog, crouching under the sink. A small dog with beady black eyes. It had white fur with black patches and a perky little tail.

Pablo smiled.

Pablo loved dogs. Especially small dogs like this one. He loved to cuddle them and tickle them and talk to them in a cutesy voice. He said, 'Hello, little doggy. Nice little doggy. What's this little doggy doing on the big scary air-oh-plane?'

The dog just stared at Pablo with a blank expression.

Pablo didn't mind. He understood that this was probably a shy little dog. He cooed, 'Come here, little doggy. Come and talk to Uncle Pablo.' He stretched out his hand to stroke the dog's head.

Grk bit him.

Pablo squealed.

He pulled his hand back. There were four little bite marks on his finger. Specks of scarlet blood bubbled through his skin.

Pablo shook his head. Yes, he liked dogs, but that didn't mean that he liked all dogs. He absolutely definitely didn't like this dog. He lunged forward with both hands, determined to grab the mutt round the neck and strangle it.

Grk jumped aside, darted between Pablo's legs and sprinted down the plane.

124

Pablo turned round and ran after him. 'Stop him!' he shouted at his brothers. 'Stop that dog!'

Grk weaved between the sacks of money, jumped over the nearest leather armchair and sprinted between José and Pelottinho. Both of them tried to grab Grk, but they were too slow.

Pablo charged down the cabin, screaming and shouting and trailing drops of blood from his damaged finger. 'Stop him! Stop him! Stop that mutt!'

José turned round and ran after Grk. After only three paces, he trod on the TV remote control. His foot slipped. The remote control shot forwards. José toppled over, waving his arms, and SMACKED his head against the edge of the sofa.

Pablo Pelotti tripped over José's outstretched legs, fell to the floor, and CRUNCHED his skull against the wall.

At the back of the cabin, Tim and Zito watched what was happening through a gap between the sacks of money. Zito started giggling. 'Sshh,' hissed Tim. But he couldn't help giggling too.

José and Pablo lay on the floor, holding their heads, groaning in agony. The only man still standing was Pelottinho. He reached into the back pocket of his jeans and took out a flick knife. He pressed a button. A sharp blade flicked open. Pelottinho took a step towards the dog, holding the knife in front of him.

Grk understand exactly what he should do next. He ran as fast as he could in the opposite direction.

Pelottinho ran after him.

125

Grk darted through the open doorway and leaped into the cockpit. Pelottinho sprinted after him, waving the knife and shouting curses in Portuguese.

The pilot couldn't believe his eyes. What was happening? A dog? A man with a knife? He had never seen anything like it. He jumped to his feet and ordered them both to get out of the cockpit. 'This is an aircraft,' he shouted. 'Not a bar. No drunks here! No knives! No fighting! And absolutely no animals! Get out and go back to your seat!'

Neither Grk nor Pelottinho took any notice of the pilot. They had more important things on their minds. Grk ran round the cockpit. Pelottinho lunged at him. The knife narrowly missed Grk's tail and plunged into the back of the pilot's seat, cutting a long tear in the leather. 'Oh my God,' shouted the pilot. 'What do you think you're doing? Are you trying to kill us all?'

Pelottinho ignored the pilot and gripped his fingers around the knife, preparing to lunge.

Grk jumped onto the control panel. He trod on the altimeter, the chronometer, the speedometer and the fuel gauge. Pelottinho thrust the knife at the dog. This time, the blade sliced through the end of Grk's tail. A few white hairs fluttered through the air.

Grk sprang across the instruments which measure air temperature and oil pressure.

Pelottinho lunged once more. His knife caught the back of Grk's leg, breaking the skin, drawing blood.

Grk jumped over the small circular piece of plastic which is designed to hold the pilot's cup of coffee and turned round. Now he wasn't scared. He was furious. He bared his teeth and growled.

The noise was enough to terrify any ordinary man. It certainly terrified the pilot. He jumped backwards, waving his arms and shouting, 'Calm down, little doggy. Keep calm.'

But there was nothing ordinary about Pelottinho, and not much scared him. He gripped his knife even more securely and lunged once more.

Grk was too quick for the one-armed man. He dodged the blade, then sprang across the cockpit with his mouth wide open and sank his teeth into Pelottinho's arm.

As you probably know, dogs have two quite different ways of biting. They can bite playfully or seriously. If they bite playfully, they just press down a little with their teeth, not breaking your skin or even hurting you very much. If you're a friend, they would only ever bite you playfully. But if you are their enemy, then they will bite you seriously, using all the strength in their jaws. They will puncture your skin and perhaps even snap your bones.

Pelottinho opened his mouth and yelled at the top of his voice. 'AAAAAHHHHH!' He dropped his knife and spun round, flapping his arm, trying to shake Grk off. Anyone else would have grabbed Grk with their other arm, but Pelottinho couldn't do that. He only had one arm, and Grk was already attached to it.

Pelottinho hurled himself against the wall of the cockpit, banging Grk against the metal, trying to knock him off. But Grk wasn't going anywhere. His teeth were firmly fastened into Pelottinho's flesh, and he had absolutely no intention of letting go.

Pelottinho's eyes bulged. The pain was unbearable. He spun round and round and round the cockpit. His elbow knocked a lever. His legs brushed three blue buttons.

A yellow light flashed. An electronic alarm started bleeping.

Grk dug his teeth even deeper into Pelottinho's arm.

Pelottinho screamed at the top of his voice. He banged into the control panel, knocking six different levers and pressing eleven buttons. The plane rocked from side to side. Another electronic alarm went off and a red sign glowed on the display.

When that happened, the pilot lunged forward, trying to reach the levers and the buttons.

But it was too late. On both wings, the flaps dropped. The plane twisted sharply to the left, rolled over, and plunged towards the earth.

Small passenger jets are designed to carry millionaires from one airport to another. They are designed to be smooth and fast and very comfortable. They are not designed to loop the loop or plunge towards the earth at great speed or perform other acrobatic manoeuvres. When they do, bad things happen.

These are some of the bad things that happened inside the plane.

The walls shuddered. The windows bulged and groaned. The fittings squealed. The leather armchairs swung round and round, threatening to come loose from their fittings. Five coffee cups crashed against the walls, smashing into fifty pieces. An English-Portuguese dictionary bounced against the floor and then against the ceiling. Forty sacks slid the length of the cabin, spilling banknotes. All the clutter that had been sitting on the table – books, bottles, magazines, spoons, plates – flew through the air like missiles.

The plane gathered speed and whizzed towards the earth. In twenty or thirty seconds, it would plunge into the ground and explode in a bright ball of flame.

Everything shook. Everything juddered.

All the people in the cabin were flung around too. Tim, Zito, José and Pablo went flying through the air just as if they were books or magazines or coffee cups.

Tim grabbed the edge of a window with both hands and clung on desperately.

I'm about to die, thought Tim.

He was surprised to notice that he didn't feel specially frightened. Actually, he felt quite calm. He didn't particularly mind the idea of dying. He just didn't want it to hurt too much.

He held on to the window and waited for the whole of his life to flash before his eyes. That was what happened just before you die. Or so he had been told.

Right now, the only thing flashing before his eyes was Zito.

Zito whizzed through the air, banging his head against the walls, his knees against the windows and his elbows against the floor. When Zito reached the end of the cabin, he smacked straight into José Pelotti. Their heads CRASHED together. They both blinked, sighed and lost consciousness.

In the cockpit, Grk, Pelottinho and the pilot were thrown together in a heap, then thrown apart again.

Grk opened his mouth and let go of Pelottinho's arm. At the same moment, Pelottinho twisted round and tried to grab Grk's tail. While that was happening, the pilot leaned forward, grabbed the lever that controlled the plane's ailerons, and pulled it.

The aircraft's nose eased round. The plane flipped over and tipped in the other direction. Rather than plunging down towards the earth, the plane was now soaring upwards.

The wings shuddered and jerked.

The engines spluttered and roared.

Inside the plane, everyone and everything flipped over too. They turned upside down, swinging desperately from side to side. Books and bodies, cups and sacks, spoons and banknotes – all of them flew through the air, banging against the windows and the walls.

The widescreen TV snapped out of its screws in the ceiling. It dropped and landed on Pablo Pelotti. He yelled in pain. Writhing on the ground, he desperately tried to free himself, but the TV was too big. Pablo lay there, pinned to the floor by an enormous television, unable to move.

If the plane had been designed for acrobatic

manoeuvres, the wings and the fuselage could have coped with such treatment. But it wasn't and they couldn't. The entire aircraft started shuddering. Screws popped out. Metal screamed. In a moment or two, one of the wings would fall off. Then the plane would drop to the ground like a stone and explode in a ball of flame.

I'm alive, thought Tim. But it's only a temporary situation. I'll probably be dead soon.

He looked around himself and tried to take stock of his situation. He was lying full-length on the side of the plane, clinging to the edge of the window. All the furnishings had been torn from their fittings. Chairs, cups and books were jumbled together in a heap, together with the contents of the forty sacks. Several sacks had exploded. It was raining money.

There were two other people alongside Tim at the back of the plane. Neither of them moved. José Pelotti lay against the wall, his eyes open, his chest still. He didn't seem to be breathing. Blood dribbled from a wound on his head. Perhaps he was dead or perhaps he was just unconscious.

Pablo Pelotti was alive and conscious, but unable to move. He was still pinned to the ground by the weight of a huge widescreen TV. With both hands, he was trying to lift the TV off his body. He struggled, pushing and straining, then flopped back, exhausted by the effort. He turned his head and stared at Tim.

Tim had never seen such hatred in another person's eyes.

Pablo said a few words in Portuguese.

Tim didn't respond in any way. When someone stares at you with such hatred, it's probably better not to talk to them. Anyway, Tim couldn't speak Portuguese.

Pablo must have realised that Tim couldn't understand him, because he said the words a second time, now in English. 'Little boy,' he hissed. His voice sounded tired. Every word was a great effort for him. 'Little... boy... I... am... kill... you.'

'You'll have to catch me first,' said Tim.

Pablo's face went bright red with fury. Making a huge effort, he tried to lift the TV off his body. His muscles bulged. His face turned bright purple. Then he fell back, unable to free himself.

'Better luck next time,' said Tim. He turned his head and gazed through the door that led to the cockpit.

Inside the cockpit, he could see the others. Pelottinho and the pilot were smeared across the control panel. The pilot was trying to regain control of the plane. He seemed to be pressing buttons and pulling levers. Tim couldn't see what Pelottinho was doing.

And what about Grk? Where was he?

Tim couldn't see him, but he suspected that Grk must be in the cockpit too.

And that was where Tim needed to be. He had to reach the cockpit. There, he would disable Pelottinho and try to help the pilot take control of the plane.

He crawled along the wall, holding the windows for support. There was no point trying to stand up, because the plane was juddering and swinging so violently from side to side. As soon as Tim got to his feet, he would be thrown down again.

He was deafened by the noise roaring through the plane. The engines were screaming. Air rushed past the windows.

As he approached the cockpit, he crawled past another limp body lying on the floor, tangled around the long leather sofa. It was Zito. He was rubbing his head with both hands and crying softly to himself.

Tim didn't have time to deal with him. That could be done later. He crawled to the end of the cabin. With one final lurch, he pulled himself into the cockpit, and landed at Pelottinho's feet.

At that precise moment, the pilot wrenched one of the levers with both hands. The plane twisted over and flipped upside-down. For an instant, everything seemed to be suspended in mid-air. Then it flipped again, twisted over and evened out.

The pilot laughed and punched the air. They were flying normally. He had regained control of the plane.

Tim was standing in the doorway. He and Pelottinho looked at one another. Neither of them moved.

Tim didn't know what to do. Should he run? Or jump at Pelottinho? Or wait until Pelottinho jumped at him?

If only I knew karate, thought Tim.

If I ever get back to London, he decided, I'm going to learn karate. And judo. And maybe some boxing too. Then if I ever again find myself stuck in a small space with a murderous criminal, I'll know what to do.

Of course, he did have one advantage: his left arm.

Both he and Pelottinho had right arms, but only Tim had a left arm. Perhaps that would help him in a fair fight.

He put up his fists.

Pelottinho smiled.

For a second, Tim felt furious. Was Pelottinho laughing at him? Was he sneering at a boy of twelve? Well, he would soon sneer on the other side of his face. He would soon understand that Tim might only be twelve, and might not know how to do karate, but he was still capable of inflicting pain.

Then he felt something touch the back of his neck. Something cold. Something metallic.

Very slowly, Tim turned round.

Pablo was standing behind him, holding a pistol. It was pointed at Tim's head. Pablo said a few words in Portuguese and made a gesture, ordering Tim to put up his hands.

Tim did as he was told.

Chapter 25

Pablo marched Tim and Zito along the length of the plane, keeping his gun trained on them. When they reached the toilet, he shoved them inside. He said something in Portuguese which Zito understood but Tim didn't, then slammed the door.

There was barely enough space for both of them. Zito put down the lid of the toilet and sat down. Tim squatted on the floor beside the basin.

Tim said, 'What did he just say? The thing he said in Portuguese. What was it?'

'Nothing important,' replied Zito.

'Even if it's not important, I'd still like to know. Tell me what he said.'

Zito sighed. 'He said he not kill us now because he not want kill us quick. He want to kill us very slow and very painful.'

'That's something to look forward to,' said Tim.

Zito looked at him, puzzled. 'I no understand.'

'It was a joke,' said Tim. 'I was just trying to be funny.'

'What is funny about painful death?'

'If you put it like that . . . not much.'

Zito sighed. He sat on the floor with his head in his hands. After a minute, his shoulders started shaking. He was crying.

Tim tried to think of something to say, but he couldn't think of anything helpful or comforting. How could he console Zito? He knew, just as Zito did, that things were looking pretty desperate. They were trapped in the back of a plane. They had no weapons. They were facing three desperate, ruthless criminals. What chance did they have?

In a minute, thought Tim, I'll probably burst into tears too.

But he didn't. He leaned against the wall and waited to see what would happen next.

Chapter 26

The jungle is never quiet. A thousand sounds are always reverberating through the air. Birds sing at the top of their voices. Monkeys gibber and shriek. Snakes hiss. Water drips. The one thing that you will never hear is silence.

On the other hand, you will rarely hear a noise as loud as the roar of a jet engine. Particularly a jet engine attached to a plane that is flying just a few feet above the tops of the trees.

The treetops shook. Birds flew out of the way. Snakes ducked for cover. Monkeys put their paws over their eyes.

The plane flew lower and lower. The undercarriage flapped open. The wheels emerged. The tyres narrowly missed the tops of the trees.

Inside the cockpit, the pilot was sweating. This was probably the most difficult landing that he had ever attempted. Fast executive jets like this one were intended for landing in big urban airports, not rough jungle landing strips. He hunched over the control panel, peering through the windscreen at the jungle below. Yes – there it was. Half a mile ahead. The landing strip. The pilot eased a lever, then clicked two switches. The plane descended a few more feet.

With a deafening roar, the plane zoomed over the

jungle, then dipped down to the landing strip. The tyres touched the earth. The plane bounced once, and once again, then bounded along the uneven ground. The Pelottis had landed.

The jet juddered to a halt. In the cockpit, the pilot wiped the sweat from his forehead.

'Congratulations,' said Pablo Pelotti, slapping him on the back. 'They were right – you are a great pilot.'

'No problem,' replied the pilot. 'I said I could do it, and I did it.'

'You did. And that's why we're paying you a million dollars.'

Chapter 27

People say that money can't buy you love. But it can buy you just about anything else.

Ten years previously, SALTCo had built a landing strip in the middle of the jungle. (As you probably know, SALTCo is the South American Logging and Timber Company. If you have a wooden table in your kitchen or a wooden floor in your hallway, the wood was probably chopped down, sawn up, shipped and sold by SALTCo) Once a week, a plane landed here. It carried some of SALTCo's employees to the jungle and returned others to the city.

Today, there wasn't a single person within ten miles of the landing strip. The Pelottis had paid all of them to keep away. Maybe money can't buy you love, but it can certainly buy you a jet plane, an experienced pilot and an empty landing strip in the middle of the jungle.

The pilot opened the jet's door and eased the flight of steps to the ground. Together, the Pelottis and the pilot unloaded the contents of the plane. First, Pablo and Pelottinho carried José down the stairs to the ground. He was semi-conscious. Pablo had wrapped some cloth around his head as a bandage.

There was a lorry parked beside the runway. The Pelottis had arranged for it to be waiting for them. The fuel tank was full. The tyres were pumped up. The keys were in the ignition.

They carried José across the runway from the plane to the lorry and laid him on the front seat.

One by one, they carried the sacks from the plane to the lorry.

When the money had been loaded onto the lorry, Pelottinho and the pilot returned to the plane. The pilot was carrying two petrol tanks that had been waiting in the back of the lorry. He unscrewed the lids, then tipped up the tanks, pouring petrol around the plane's undercarriage, soaking the soil and the grass and the rubber tyres. One spark would be enough to turn the plane into a blazing inferno.

The pilot dropped both petrol cans and wiped his hands on his trousers. He turned to look at Pelottinho. 'Well, that's that. Do you have a match?'

'No.'

'No? Then how are we going to light the fire?'

'I have this,' said Pelottinho. He reached into the back of his jeans and pulled out a pistol.

'You can't light a fire with a pistol.'

'Of course you can't,' said Pelottinho, smiling as if the pilot had said something completely ridiculous. 'Well, I've enjoyed our little chat, but now it's time to go. Thank you for all your work. And goodbye.'

The pilot looked surprised. 'Goodbye? What do you mean, goodbye?'

'When I say goodbye, I mean goodbye.'

The pilot shook his head. 'I don't understand. Are you

leaving me here?'

'The lorry has three seats,' said Pelottinho. He spoke in a slow, calm voice as if he was talking to an idiot. 'There are three Pelotti brothers. There is Pablo. There is José. And there is Pelottinho. One for each seat. Where would you sit?'

'What about my money?'

'What about your money?'

'You promised me a million dollars,' said the pilot. 'We agreed a fee for flying from Rio to here. I want to be paid.'

'You won't need money where you're going,' said Pelottinho.

The pilot said, 'What is that supposed to mean?'

'Isn't it obvious?' Pelottinho swung his arm and whacked the pilot's forehead with the pistol, knocking him out instantly. The pilot fell to the ground and lay there, not moving.

Pelottinho tucked his pistol into the back of his jeans. He reached into his pocket and pulled out a silver lighter. 'Goodbye,' he whispered. 'Goodbye, little dog. Goodbye, little boys.' He flicked the lighter. A flame spurted. He dropped the lighter into the pool of petrol, then turned and ran back to the lorry.

The petrol flared up immediately. Flames licked the grass, the plane and the pilot's boots.

Pablo was already revving the lorry's engine. Pelottinho swung himself into the cab and slammed the door.

As bright scarlet flames engulfed the plane, the three Pelotti brothers drove into the jungle.

141

Chapter 28

Tim sat up slowly, blinking and groaning. His head ached. He rubbed his hands over his face and scalp, checking for blood. There didn't seem to be any. Nothing was broken.

He sniffed the air. What was that? He could smell something. It was acrid and bitter. He sniffed again, taking deep breaths. Yes – he could definitely smell burning.

Zito was still lying on the floor, rubbing his head, groaning gently to himself.

'Get up,' shouted Tim. 'Get up! We're going to be burnt alive!'

Zito turned his head slowly from side to side, making no effort to move, as if he didn't understand what Tim was talking about.

One thing at a time, thought Tim. First, find a way out. Then deal with Zito. Every second, the smell of smoke was growing stronger. The air felt hot. The plane must be burning. If they didn't get out soon, they would be barbecued like sausages.

Tim turned the door handle. To his surprise, the door opened. It wasn't locked. He stepped into the cabin. Immediately, he stumbled backwards, knocked almost to his knees by a dense wave of black smoke. He started coughing. The thick smoke made breathing impossible.

He wouldn't be able to get to the other end of the plane without choking to death.

But if he didn't open the door or break a window, he would be fried alive. Scarlet flames were licking the walls. Smoke was trickling up through the carpet.

Coughing and choking, Tim retreated back into the toilet and closed the door, blocking out the smoke.

Zito was sitting on the floor, shaking his head in terror. 'We die, we die,' moaned Zito. 'We are dead.'

'No, we're not,' said Tim. 'Not yet.' He pulled off his T-shirt. 'Turn on the tap.'

'Why?'

'Just do it.'

Zito stared at him, surprised by the curt tone of Tim's voice. He was about to say something. Then he thought better of it. He got to his feet and turned on the tap in the basin. Cold water gushed out.

'Now, take off your T-shirt,' said Tim.

Zito did as he was told. They were both bare-chested.

Tim dropped the two T-shirts under the tap. When the material was thoroughly soaked, Tim pulled them out and handed one to Zito. 'Cover your mouth and your nose,' he said. 'Like this.' He placed his own T-shirt over his face, blocking his mouth and nose. 'And keep close to the floor. That's where the clean air is.'

Zito did exactly as he was instructed.

Tim led the way, opening the door, ducking down and crawling along the floor of the plane.

In a fire, you should always cover your mouth and nose with a wet cloth. Tim knew that from a special fire-fighting class at school. From the same class, he also knew how to put out a fire in a chip pan and how to tell if the battery in a fire detector has run out. Neither of those skills were much help in the present situation.

He could feel the fire on his bare chest. It felt like the sun at midday, but multiplied a thousand times.

This is how roast chickens must feel, thought Tim. But at least chickens don't get roasted alive.

They crawled along the floor and reached the door. Tim turned the handle. It was locked. He shook the handle, then pushed and pulled with all his strength, but he was too weak. They were locked inside. With every second that passed, the cabin was hotter and the smoke was thicker.

'We are dead,' moaned Zito in a piteous voice. 'We are dead.'

This time, Tim ignored him. He didn't want to waste his breath replying. He knew that they didn't have much time: the flames would soon reach the plane's fuel tank. When that happened, all the fuel would explode, creating an inferno that nothing could possibly survive.

He saw something moving. A ball of white. Running along the floor towards him. 'Grk,' called Tim. 'You're alive!'

Grk sprinted towards him, barking joyfully. But his barks soon turned to coughs as smoke filled his lungs.

The three of them lay on the ground, trying to suck a few breaths of clean air into their lungs.

Tim looked around. What could he do? The door was locked. The windows were constructed from toughened glass. There was no way that he could smash through them. The windscreen was the same. How could they get out?

Every second, the smoke was thicker. The damp cloth provided little protection. Tim could feel the lack of oxygen in his lungs. I'm going to die, he thought. I'm going to suffocate. And even if I don't suffocate, the flames are going to reach the fuel tanks and the plane is going to explode in a blazing ball of flame. I'm going to die.

Then a vision flashed before his eyes. It wasn't a vision of his life, like people said you saw just before you died. It was a vision of a movie that he'd once seen. It was an American movie that had been on TV one night when his parents went to the theatre. The babysitter was supposed to send him to bed at 8.30, but she let him stay up and watch the movie with her. Some terrorists took over a Boeing 747. The hero found a hatch in the floor and climbed down to the cargo compartments.

A hatch in the floor. But where?

Tim crawled along the floor. He spread his arms, feeling the surface with his fingers. From the other end of the plane, he could hear desperate coughs. Was that Grk? Or Zito? He couldn't tell. He tried to ignore the noise and concentrated on searching the floor.

He ran his hands along the walls. He swept his fingers across the middle of the floor. He touched smooth metal. Nothing else. There was no hatch.

So what could he do?

Nothing. There was nothing he could do.

There was no way out of the plane. There was no oxygen left. Tim could feel his lungs protesting desperately as smoke filled every crevice. He was lying on the floor of the plane, gasping for breath, without success. His lungs felt as if they were slowly being filled with concrete. All the energy was seeping out of his body. He couldn't breathe, couldn't think, couldn't move. This is it, he thought. This is the end.

Chapter 29

The door swung open. A blast of fresh air swept into the cabin. A pair of strong hands grabbed Tim, pulled him to his feet and thrust him out of the plane.

Tim stumbled onto the grass, fell over, then picked himself up again and turned round, only to see Zito flying through the door, arms flailing, and landing on the grass beside him. They were joined by Grk, then the pilot, who shouted in Portuguese, waving his arms and pointing at the trees that lined the landing strip. Tim couldn't understand what the pilot was saying, but he knew exactly what he meant: the plane was just about to blow up.

The four of them stumbled away from the burning wreckage and headed for the shelter of the trees.

With a roar, the plane exploded.

The force of the blast knocked them to the ground.

A ball of smoke wafted into the air.

All around the jungle, animals and birds ducked for cover, terrified by the noise that had shattered their peaceful existence. Monkeys hollered. Parrots shrieked. Antelopes ran. Jaguars flinched. Toucans twittered. Armadillos shrank into their shells.

Debris scattered in every direction. Flaming pieces of metal crashed through the branches and splattered down on the ground like huge smoking hailstones.

Chapter 30

Half a mile away, the Pelottis' truck was driving along a bumpy track. On either side of the road, the jungle was so thick that you couldn't see further than a few feet. Toucans and monkeys sat in the trees, staring in surprise at the unexpected sight of a vehicle. They didn't often see anyone driving along this road.

With no warning, a huge explosion rocked the air.

The air seemed to move backwards and forwards for a second. The lorry juddered, rattling the windscreen.

Pablo Pelotti put his foot on the brake. The truck stopped. Both doors opened. Pablo and Pelottinho jumped out. They left José inside, still semi-conscious, slumped on the seat.

Pablo and Pelottinho stood in the middle of the track. Above the top of the trees, they could see a thick column of black smoke spiralling into the blue sky.

Pablo said, 'That's that. We'll never see those two boys again.'

'Or that stupid little dog,' added Pelottinho.

Pablo glanced at his right hand. The wounds had healed, but he could still see the four marks made by Grk's teeth. 'I hope his death was painful,' said Pablo.

'And slow,' added Pelottinho.

Pablo and Pelottinho stood there for a minute with big grins on their faces, enjoying the thought of Tim and

Zito and Grk in a thousand tiny pieces. Pablo chuckled. Pelottinho chortled. Then they turned round, strolled back to the truck and clambered inside. Pablo started the engine and they continued driving through the jungle.

Chapter 31

Tim coughed and retched. His throat felt as if he had swallowed broken glass. His lungs ached. His hair was burnt and his skin was blackened. But he was alive.

He sat up and looked around.

Grk and Zito were lying on one side of him. The pilot lay on the other.

Tim leaned over to the pilot. In a loud voice, pronouncing every syllable slowly and carefully, he said, 'Sir? Excuse me? Do ... you ... speak ... English?'

'Sure I do,' said the pilot. 'I've spoken it all my life.'

Tim was surprised. 'Are you from England?'

'No, mate. Australia. Born and bred in Wagga Wagga.'

'Wagga Wagga,' said Tim, trying not to laugh. 'Is that a real place?'

'Yeah, it's a lovely little town,' said the pilot. 'Halfway between Sydney and Melbourne. My mum and dad still live there. You couldn't ask for a nicer place to raise a family.'

'Then what are you doing here?'

'I've been living here in Brazil for the past ten years. Flying planes. I prefer the climate. Bit too hot back home. In more ways than one.' The pilot grinned and leaned over, offering his hand. 'My name's Shane, by the way.'

'I'm Tim.'

'Pleased to meet you, Tim.'

They shook hands.

'Thank you for saving our lives,' said Tim.

'That's no problem.' Shane grinned. 'If I'd known those guys were going to kill us, I'd never have taken this job in the first place.'

'But you must have known who they were,' said Tim. 'You must have recognised them. You knew they were bank robbers, didn't you?'

Shane looked nervous for a moment. 'You're not the police, are you?'

Tim said, 'Do I look like a policeman?'

Shane took a long, hard look at Tim, then shook his head. 'Not much, mate. You're a bit small.'

'I'm only twelve,' said Tim.

'No worries. I've had a few brushes with the law, that's all. They never seem to see my good side. Anyway, yes, you're right. I knew these guys were up to no good. But I'm like any other working man. I needed the money.'

'You trusted them?'

Shane shrugged his shoulders. 'That's pretty stupid, right?'

'Right,' said Tim.

Shane explained what had happened. A week ago, he had been sitting in a bar in Rio, drinking his fourteenth beer of the night, when a man took the seat beside him, bought him beer number fifteen and offered him a job. All he had to do was fly from Rio to a landing strip in

151

the jungle. For that, he would be paid a million dollars.

Six years ago, Shane had worked for SALTCo, so he knew this area and had often landed small planes right here on this landstrip. 'For that kind of money, I'll sell my grandmother,' said Shane. 'Actually, I'd sell her for a lot less.'

He explained what had happened since the plane landed. He had been knocked out by Pelottinho and left to burn beside the petrol-drenched plane. When he regained consciousness, he remembered the two boys trapped inside the plane and decided to rescue them. 'Just in time too,' he said. 'A few more seconds and we'd all have been barbied.'

When you have been locked inside a toilet for two hours, then poisoned by smoke, burnt by flames and showered with bits of an exploding aeroplane, you could be forgiven for wanting a quick snooze. Grk and Zito stretched full-length on the ground and closed their eyes, determined to get their strength back by sleeping for a few minutes. But they hadn't reckoned with Tim. Clapping his hands together, he harangued them at the top of his voice. 'Come on!' he shouted. 'Get up! On your feet! We have to hurry.'

Grk opened his right eye, looked at Tim for a second, then shut his eye again.

Zito didn't bother opening either of his eyes. He just mumbled, 'Go way. Go way.'

'Come on.' Tim clapped his hands again. 'Get up! Time to move!'

'Noooo,' groaned Zito. 'I be tired. I sleep now.'

'You can sleep later.' Tim crouched down on the ground and shook Zito's shoulder. 'Come on, get up. We have things to do.'

'What things?' asked Zito, yawning and rubbing his eyes.

'We have to chase the Pelottis. They're getting away. We have to stop them.'

When Zito heard that, he shook his head. 'Oh, no, no, no. I never see them again! Never ever! They kill me. And they kill you too. If we be lucky, we never ever see those Pelottis in our lives.'

'We came here to stop them,' said Tim. 'And we're going to stop them.'

'No, no, no.' Zito closed his eyes and lay down to sleep again. Through half-closed lips, he mumbled, 'I stay here. Good night.'

Tim didn't know what to do. He looked at Shane, who was standing up, inspecting the smouldering holes in his uniform. But before Tim could even ask the question, Shane shook his head. 'Sorry, mate. No can do. The Pelottis have already tried to kill me once today. That's once too much. I'm not going anywhere near them.'

'Fine,' said Tim. 'I'll go on my own.'

Then he remembered Grk. Of course, he wouldn't really be alone. He would be accompanied by the bravest, cleverest little white dog on the planet.

And then he thought of something else. He kneeled down beside Zito and whispered in a low voice, 'What about the reward?'

153

Zito opened his eyes. 'Reward? What reward?'

'The reward that the police will pay to whoever captures the Pelotti brothers. They've offered a reward of one million dollars for each brother.'

Zito thought for a minute. He scratched his head. He said, 'One million?'

'Each. Dead or alive.'

'One million for Pablo and one million for José and one million for Pelottinho?'

'Precisely,' said Tim.

Zito thought about this for a second. 'Three million dollars,' he muttered with a low, admiring whistle. He jumped to his feet and rubbed his hands together. 'Okay! We catch them! What we wait for?' He looked around the jungle, staring at the trees and creepers as if he would actually be able to see the Pelottis. 'Which way they go?'

'This way,' said Tim. He had already spotted the lorry's tyre tracks leading across the flattened grass and heading down a road that led through the jungle. He glanced at Shane. 'Sure you don't want to come too? You can have a third of the money. That's one million dollars.'

'No, thank you,' said Shane. 'If you want to be a hero, be a hero on your own. I'm not interested.'

'More money for us,' said Zito. 'Come, Tim, come. Come, little Grk. Time to go. Time for making some monies.' Rubbing his hands together, gleefully imagining how he would spend three million dollars, Zito hurried across the runway and headed down the track that led into the jungle.

Tim and Grk hurried behind him, jogging to keep up.

Creepers hung down from the trees. The air was dark and musty. Strange sounds echoed. There were sudden flashes of colour as multi-coloured butterflies fluttered through the air. Bright green parrots flew overhead, swooping from tree to tree. Tim had the sense that he was being watched, but he couldn't see anything or anyone watching him.

Both Tim and Zito were wearing their damp T-shirts. The cloth stank of smoke. If they had been walking in sunshine, the heat would have dried their T-shirts in a few minutes, but here, shaded by the thick net of leaves and creepers, they stayed wet.

Tim felt a little guilty. He had lied to Zito. He had invented the fact that the police were offering one million dollars per brother, dead or alive. He did know that the police were offering a reward for the capture of the Pelotti brothers, but he didn't know exactly how much it would be.

But if he hadn't lied, Zito would still be lying on the grass, snoozing, and they would have no chance of catching the Pelottis.

What was worse: lying and catching the Pelottis? Or telling the truth and losing them?

Lying is wrong. Tim knew that. But sometimes you have to lie or something even worse will happen.

A hundred different extraordinary sounds filled the air. Shrieks. Mutterings. Wailing. Yells. Some of the sounds were creepy and frightening, sending shivers running up and down Tim's spine. Others just sounded weird. At one moment, there was a low roar like distant thunder. A little later, there was a *snap-snap-snappity-snap-snappity-snap-snap* which sounded like fifty flamenco dancers clicking their castanets. What could possibly be making all these different sounds. Animals? Birds? Reptiles?

They had been walking for an hour or two when Zito stopped and pointed up at the trees. 'Look,' he said. 'There! You see?'

Tim stared, following the direction that Zito was pointing. For a moment, he couldn't see anything other than branches and leaves and creepers. Then his eyes adjusted, and he made out three monkeys squatting in the branches, high up in the trees. A fourth was hanging upside-down by his tail, grabbing big handfuls of leaves and stuffing them into his mouth. They didn't seem to be frightened of humans – they took no notice of Tim and Zito – perhaps because so few humans ventured out here, deep in the jungle, many miles from the nearest village.

'Come on,' said Tim. 'We have to hurry. We'll never catch them if we stand around all day looking at monkeys.'

Zito shook his head. 'We never catch them anyway,' he sighed. All his enthusiasm had faded. The thought of three million dollars no longer filled him with energy. 'They have truck. We walk. Too slow. Impossible to catch.'

'We can try,' said Tim. 'Come on, let's walk fast.' He tugged Zito's arm and persuaded him to keep walking along the uneven track.

Deep down, Tim knew that Zito was probably right. In their truck, the Pelottis should be able to drive at ten or fifteen miles an hour, even on this bumpy road. Tim, Zito and Grk wouldn't be able to walk more than two or three miles an hour. Every minute, they were dropping further behind.

Perhaps it was hopeless to try and catch the Pelottis. Perhaps they should have stayed with the burning aircraft, waiting for someone to come and rescue them. But Tim didn't just want to sit and wait. He wasn't prepared to give up yet. He put his head down and walked as fast as he could. Behind him, Zito and Grk hurried to keep up.

They had been walking for several hours when they heard the sound of an engine. It came from behind them, back in the direction of the landing strip. Tim briefly wondered whether they should hide in the jungle, then decided not. Perhaps the vehicle would be driven by the army or the police. If so, they could get a lift.

They stood in the middle of the track, listening to the engine get louder and louder.

A white Land Rover turned the corner. SALTCo was painted on the bonnet and the doors in big black letters. The Land Rover reached the two boys, then stopped.

Shane leaned out of the window and grinned. He was sitting in the driver's seat. Somewhere, he had found his pilot's cap, and he was wearing it at a crooked angle. He said, 'Fancy a lift, guys?'

Tim looked at him. 'Where are you going?'

'To catch the Pelottis. Want to come too?'

'Sure,' said Tim.

Zito, Grk and Tim clambered into the Land Rover. Tim and Grk sat in the front alongside Shane, while Zito had the whole of the back seat to himself.

Shane explained that, after they went into the jungle, leaving him alone, he had started thinking. He thought about what Tim had said. He thought about the actions of Pelottinho. He thought about the million dollars that they had promised to pay him. And he thought about Pelottinho's attempt to kill him. When he had thought through all these factors, he changed his mind. 'You were right,' said Shane. 'I don't want those cheating Pelottis to get away with this.'

He used to work for SALTCo, so he knew where they hid their spare vehicles. He had found the Land Rover, fully loaded with petrol, covered with a tarpaulin and parked in the jungle at the far end of the landing strip.

The Pelottis were driving a heavy lorry loaded with forty sacks. The Land Rover was much lighter and much faster. With any luck, they should be able to overtake the Pelottis' lorry before nightfall.

'Then let's go,' said Tim.

Shane grinned. 'Hey, kiddo, I like your attitude. Hang on tight.' He revved the engine and accelerated into the jungle.

Chapter 32

Shane was the first to hear it. He stopped the Land Rover and turned off the engine. 'Listen,' he said. 'You know what that is?'

They had been driving for several hours, and the two boys had fallen asleep while Shane concentrated on the road ahead. Zito was sprawled across the long seat in the back. Tim was slumped on the front seat with Grk snoring and dribbling on his lap.

'Boys, wake up,' said Shane. 'Can you hear it?'

Zito sat up, groaning and blinking and stretching his arms.

Tim rubbed his eyes and said, 'Hear what?'

'Ssshh,' said Shane. 'Just listen.'

They sat and listened. Even Grk cocked his head on one side and lifted his ears.

Without the sound of the engine to drown out all the jungle's other noises, they could hear birds squealing in the trees and monkeys chattering and insects whirring and water dripping and frogs chirruping. But they could also hear something else.

Tim said, 'What is it?'

Shane smiled. 'Can't you guess?'

'No.'

'Listen. Just listen.'

'I am listening.'

'Listen harder.'

Tim closed his eyes and listened and tried to work out what he was hearing.

If you had heard that noise for a few seconds, you might have guessed that it was thunder. But unlike thunder, it didn't have a beginning or an end, it just continued all the time. Like the noise of machinery grinding away in a factory. Or the hum of a jet plane preparing to take off. Or a distant roll of drums which never started and never stopped.

Tim opened his eyes. 'I don't know. What is it?'

Shane looked at Zito. 'How about you? Know what that is?'

'I not know,' said Zito, shaking his head slowly from side to side. 'Maybe machine? Big machine?'

'No, mate,' said Shane. 'That's not a machine. That is one hundred per cent pure natural noise. What you're hearing there is the Machado Falls. I reckon they're the biggest waterfalls in South America. Maybe even the biggest in the world. You never seen them?'

Zito and Tim both admitted that they had not.

'They're an amazing sight,' said Shane. 'Truly amazing. More water than I've ever seen in my life. Pouring over this huge drop. It's, like, totally beautiful. But I've got to tell you something else. We'll have to get hold of those Pelotti brothers pretty darn soon or they're gonna be gone forever. Upstream of the falls, there's two thousand miles of rivers. Twisting and turning. All kinds of little inlets and islands. Most of them aren't even shown on a map. If

160

the Pelottis get into that, no one will find them in a million years.'

They left the Land Rover and walked the last section of the track, not wanting the Pelottis to hear the engine.

Shane led the way, striding quickly along the path. Tim and Zito hurried to keep up with him. Grk lingered behind, stopping often to sniff interesting scents, then bounding after the others, wagging his tail.

They reached the riverbank and squatted down on the ground, keeping themselves shielded behind the trees and bushes. Slowly, carefully, Shane nudged forward through the undergrowth, pushing aside the thick net of leaves and branches. The others followed him. Tim grabbed Grk's collar and whispered, 'Stay with me. Understand?'

Grk wagged his tail. He was having fun.

Shane beckoned. They crouched down on the damp earth and peered through a gap in the branches.

The first thing they saw was Pablo Pelotti, carrying one of the brown sacks filled with money.

Pablo walked up a long, silver gangplank and into a big white boat. It was a motor cruiser, about fifty feet long, with round portholes running along the side. Two strong ropes tethered the cruiser to the shore. Each rope was tied around the trunk of a palm tree.

Pablo carried the sack onto the cruiser and disappeared through a doorway. A minute later, he reappeared, hurried down the gangplank, returned to the lorry and collected another sack.

161

'There, look.' Tim nudged Shane. 'Do you see?' He pointed at the cruiser's cabin.

Pelottinho was standing in the cabin, peering at the river through a pair of binoculars. Beside him, José was sitting in a high-backed chair. Wrapped around his skull, José wore a white bandage, speckled with spots of blood.

In whispers, Tim, Shane and Zito discussed what to do.

'Is three against three,' said Zito. 'But they has guns.'

'Four against three.' Tim gestured at Grk. 'There are four of us.'

'I don't want to offend your dog, mate,' said Shane. 'But I can't imagine him being that much help.' Shane sighed. 'One man, two boys and a dog against the three most dangerous criminals in South America. What hope do we have?'

Tim looked at him. 'So, what do you suggest?'

'I don't know, mate. Call the cops?'

'We don't have a radio.'

'That's true.' Shane bit his lower lip, then shook his head. 'I really don't know, mate. Sorry. You got any ideas?'

Tim nodded. Quickly, he explained his idea. Zito and Shane waited till he had finished. Then both of them shook their heads.

'Sounds much too dangerous,' said Shane.

'Is not good,' agreed Zito.

Tim looked at them. 'Do either of you have a better plan?'

Neither of them did.

There was only one route from the shore to the boat: straight up the gangplank. As soon as Pablo ducked into the doorway, carrying another sack of money, Tim pushed aside the undergrowth and started running. He sprinted across the grass and up the gangplank. Grk disobeyed all the instructions that he had been given and ran after him. Both of them arrived on the deck of the cruiser, turned left, ducked and hid behind the rubber dinghy. It wasn't a very good hiding-place, but there was nowhere better.

At that moment, Pablo emerged from the doorway and walked down the gangplank.

In the undergrowth, Zito and Shane waited. They had arranged that Zito would go next. Then Shane. Once all four of them had taken up their positions on the boat, they would get rid of the gangplank, trapping Pablo on the shore. That would leave one man, two boys and a dog to fight against a man with concussion and a man with one arm. It wasn't the best odds in the world but, with a little bit of luck, it could probably be done.

Zito tensed his muscles, preparing to run, waiting for Pablo to turn his back.

Pablo walked along the shore and stopped beside the palm tree to which one of the ropes had been tied. He hunched over the knot, then unlooped the rope and threw it aboard the cruiser. He walked along the shore to the second tree and the second rope.

Shane and Zito stared at one another. To their horror,

they realised what was happening.

The Pelottis had loaded all the money onto their cruiser. Now, they were leaving. With Tim and Grk aboard.

Shane and Zito couldn't move from the shelter of the undergrowth without being seen. There was nothing they could do except sit there and watch helplessly as Pablo untied the second rope, then walked up the gangplank and pulled it after him. In the cabin, Pelottinho revved the engine and turned the steering wheel. The cruiser eased slowly away from the shore and joined the fast-flowing river. Pablo stowed the gangplank and clambered up the stairs to the cabin, where he joined his two brothers. The three of them stared forward at the river ahead.

Back on the shore, Shane muttered, 'What are we going to do now? Any ideas, mate?'

Zito shook his head slowly from side to side.

Together, the two of them stared hopelessly at the white cruiser as it chugged into the middle of the current and disappeared around the first curve in the river.

Chapter 33

For a minute, Tim was paralysed by fear and indecision. He was trapped on a fifty-foot boat with three dangerous criminals. They had guns and knifes; he had nothing. What could he do?

He looked at the rubber dinghy behind which he had hidden. Perhaps he could unlash the ropes and toss it overboard. He and Grk could leap into the dinghy and paddle safely to the shore.

But that would leave the Pelottis to escape with forty sacks stuffed with cash.

He had chased them all the way from Rio to the jungle. They had tried to kill him. He wasn't going to give up now.

So what else could he do?

If only I had a gun, thought Tim. Or a mobile phone. Or a knife. Or anything at all. But all I have is me and Grk.

How could he stop the Pelottis?

Stop them.

Yes, he thought. That's it. I have to *stop* them.

He leaned down and whispered to Grk, 'You stay here. Understand? Stay. Stay!'

Grk wagged his tail.

Tim shuffled out of his hiding-place and started crawling along the deck.

Grk padded after him.

Tim turned round. 'No,' he hissed. 'Hide! Stay! I'm going alone.'

Grk's tail wagged cheerily. Grk knew they were playing some kind of game. He didn't completely understand the rules, but he was enjoying it. He put his head on one side, stared at Tim and waited to see what would happen next.

'Oh, all right then,' whispered Tim. 'Come too.'

Tim crawled along the deck on his hands and knees. Over the noise of the motor, he could hear the Pelottis talking. He peered around the corner.

There they were – the three brothers – sitting in the cabin, staring at the river ahead. If any of them turned around, they would see Tim.

He sneaked through the doorway and hurried down the stairs. Grk sprinted after him.

At the bottom of the stairs, Tim and Grk found themselves in a slim, elegant room. Long white leather sofas lined the walls. There was a small fridge, a large TV, a bunch of flowers in a glass vase and a wooden coffee table. A plate of biscuits sat in the middle of the coffee table. It looked just like a posh sitting room in an urban flat.

Through the round portholes, Tim could see the river whizzing past. He noticed a huge white bird – a heron, perhaps – flapping its wide wings and flying just above the surface of the water.

'Right,' said Tim. 'Which way is the engine?'

Grk didn't answer. He was sniffing the plate of

biscuits. He had suddenly remembered that he hadn't eaten all day.

Three doors led off the room. Tim opened the first and found a small kitchen. He opened the second and discovered a bedroom. He opened the third. A corridor led down into the bowels of the boat.

Tim hurried down the corridor.

Grk followed, leaving a trail of biscuit crumbs.

Tim could hear the noise of the engine, chugging and roaring. He pushed open one door, then another, and finally found himself in the engine room.

He had no idea what to do next. He wished that Shane was there. Shane was a pilot. Shane would know how to stop an engine. Shane would know exactly which lever to pull or which button to press. But Tim didn't have a clue. He stared at the pounding engine and the pumping levers and the whirring gears, and wondered what to do.

There was only one way to find out.

A bag of tools was tucked under a shelf. Tim searched through the bag and found a crowbar. It was black and heavy and about two feet long. He gripped it with both hands. Using all his strength, he rammed the crowbar into the middle of the engine, then jumped backwards.

The bar bent. Gears snapped. Metal screamed. Bright red sparks sprayed into the air. There was a roar and a crunch and a sound like breaking glass. Levers stopped pumping. Wheels stopped turning. Gears disengaged. And then there was nothing except silence.

*

167

In the cabin, the three Pelottis looked at one another.

Without the *chug-chug-chug-chug* of the engine, the atmosphere was eerily quiet. The only sound was the water slapping against the sides of the boat.

Pablo fiddled with the controls, pulling levers and pressing buttons, trying to restart the engine, but nothing happened.

The boat slowed, then stopped. It paused for a moment in mid-stream, as if deciding which way to go. Then the current caught it. Slowly at first, but quicker with every passing second, the cruiser travelled backwards. Soon, it would pass the landing-stage where Shane and Zito were waiting. A minute or two after that, it would reach the Machado Falls. And then there would be only one possible outcome: the cruiser would tip over the edge of the foaming waterfall, drop a hundred feet and crash at the bottom in a thousand pieces.

Pablo yelled at his brothers, giving them instructions. He ordered José to stay in the cabin and try to steer them away from the waterfalls. He ordered Pelottinho to check every room on the cruiser for stowaways. And he himself ran down the stairs to the engine room.

Tim hid behind the white leather sofa. He heard thundering feet on the stairs. He waited until Pablo headed down the corridor towards the engine room. Then he crept across the cabin. In his right hand, he was holding a spanner that he had taken from the tool bag. He emerged in the bright sunlight and ran up the staircase that led up to the cabin.

José Pelotti was sitting in the high-backed leather chair, both hands clasped around the steering wheel. Hearing footsteps, he turned round. When he saw Tim, his eyes widened. His face contorted with fury.

Tim said, 'Don't move. Stay sitting down or I'll hit you.'

José jumped to his feet. He lifted his hands and clenched his fists.

'I'm warning you,' said Tim. 'If you come one step closer, I'll hit you.'

José took a step towards Tim. He smiled – an evil, vicious smile.

Tim clasped the spanner with both hands. He felt terrified. 'Not another step,' he said. 'Don't move! Don't come any closer.'

José opened his mouth and let out a fierce, inarticulate roar of rage. He ran towards Tim, waving his arms.

Tim didn't know what to do. Should he run? Try to hide? Jump out of the way? In the end, he didn't have time or space to do anything except lunge desperately at José with the spanner.

The end of the spanner smacked against José's skull.

José stopped still. His eyeballs rolled in their sockets. He staggered backwards, swayed to and fro, then collapsed on the floor.

'Sorry,' said Tim. 'I hope that didn't hurt too much.'

There were two reasons why José didn't answer. Firstly, he couldn't speak English. Secondly, he was unconscious.

Tim looked up.

The wheel was spinning. No one was controlling the cruiser's direction. That allowed the current to take it. And the current chose to take it directly towards the Machado Falls.

Pablo stood in the engine room, staring at the smoking ruins of the engine. He could see that someone had deliberately stuffed the crowbar into the middle of the gears and levers. A saboteur must have boarded the boat.

Then he saw something else.

On the floor, there was a trail of biscuit crumbs.

He followed them.

Tim stood in the cabin. José lay on the floor at his feet. The wheel spun. They were heading towards the waterfalls. The noise of roaring water grew louder every second.

He didn't know what to do. Should he try to steer the boat? Should he jump into the water? He wouldn't be strong enough to swim against the current. But what else could he do?

He remembered the rubber dinghy, strapped to the rails. If he could get that, he might be able to paddle to the shore. Of course, the current could still sweep him over the waterfall. But it was worth trying.

Before he could make a move, Pablo's head appeared at the top of the stairs.

They stared at one another.

'Hello,' said Tim.

Pablo didn't reply. Perhaps he was too surprised to

speak. He certainly couldn't believe what he was seeing. The last he knew, Tim had been locked in a burning plane.

Tim said, 'Lovely weather, isn't it?'

Pablo still didn't reply. He looked at Tim, then glanced at José's motionless body, sprawled on the floor. He climbed the last of the stairs and stood in the cabin. He reached behind his back and grabbed the pistol that was tucked into his jeans.

Pablo and Tim stood a few feet apart, facing one another. Tim was holding a spanner and Pablo was holding a pistol. No contest. Pablo lifted the pistol and pointed it at Tim's head. 'Drop that,' he said. 'Now.'

Tim did as he was told. He opened his fingers, releasing the spanner. It bounced on the floor.

Pablo nodded. 'Good boy.'

Tim knew that he had to move fast. In a few seconds, Pelottinho would climb the stairs. Then there would be two Pelottis against one of him. He wouldn't be able to do anything.

But he also knew something else. Behind Pablo, he could see the lip of the waterfalls, only two or three hundred yards away. The boat was rushing towards the edge. But something blocked their path. Between the boat and the waterfalls, there was an outcrop of sharp rocks, covered in slimy green moss.

The boat was heading straight for them.

If Pablo turned round, he would see the rocks.

Tim had to stop him from turning round. Just for a few seconds. That would be enough. The cruiser would

171

continue on its path and smash straight into those rocks. Then the Pelottis wouldn't be going anywhere.

Speaking in a loud, clear, confident voice, Tim said, 'Give me the pistol.'

Pablo looked confused. 'What you say?'

'Give me the pistol. Right now.'

'Or what will you do?'

'I will cause you a lot of pain.'

Pablo laughed. 'And how, little boy? How you pain me?'

'Like this,' said Tim. He whistled.

Grk knew exactly what to do. He leaped forward, opened his mouth as wide as he could, clamped his teeth around Pablo's ankle and bit with all his strength.

Pablo twisted on the spot, screaming and waving his arms. He pointed the pistol at the ground. But he couldn't shoot at Grk without firing a bullet into his own foot.

Tim ducked down and grabbed the spanner. He lifted it in the air. With all his strength, he bashed it against the back of Pablo's leg.

Pablo yelled and stumbled backwards. He swung the pistol round. Now it was pointing at Tim's head. Pablo's mouth lifted in a cruel smile. His finger tightened on the trigger and there was an almighty CRAAAAAASHHH.

This is it, thought Tim. I'm dead.

He waited to see what would happen next. Would everything go dark? Would he see the glittering gates of heaven? Would he spend some time as a ghost? Or a zombie?

Then he thought, this is strange. I'm dead, but it doesn't feel any different to being alive.

And then he realised that he wasn't dead. The crash hadn't been the sound of the bullet leaving the gun. It was the sound of the cruiser ramming into the rock.

The impact threw Pablo backwards. He flipped over the balustrade. The gun went flying. Waving his arms and screaming, Pablo swooped through the air and thumped on the lower deck in a heap, trapping his right leg under his body. With a loud SNAP, his leg broke in three places. Pablo lay there, groaning in agony, unable to move.

Tim was sprawled on the floor. His head hurt. He felt like going to sleep. But he knew that he had to get off the boat. It was tipping over onto its side. The rocks had made a long gaping hole in the fibreglass. Water was pouring in.

'Come on,' hissed Tim. 'Let's go!' He beckoned to Grk. Together, they sprinted down the stairs, ran along the deck and reached the rubber dinghy. It was attached to the rails with a thick rope. Tim tried to untie the knots, but his fingers were shaking so much that he made little progress.

'Boy!' said a loud voice.

Tim turned around.

Pelottinho was standing a few feet away. In his hand, he was holding a flick knife. He lunged.

Tim jumped backwards. The knife missed his stomach by six inches.

Pelottinho lunged again.

Tim jumped back. This time, the tip of the knife cut a slit in his T-shirt. Another inch and his belly would have been sliced open.

Tim knew that he only had one chance. Pelottinho's next lunge would kill him. So he leaned down, grabbed Grk in his arms and jumped off the boat into the water. Immediately, the current took hold of Tim and Grk, rolling them over, sweeping them towards the edge of the Machado Falls.

Pelottinho gripped his knife between his teeth, dived off the edge of the boat and swam after them.

Chapter 34

The roar of water was louder than a jet engine. Even if Tim hadn't been holding Grk, he wouldn't have been strong enough to swim against the current. He just tried to keep his and Grk's mouths above the water as they swooshed towards the edge.

It was fifty feet away. Now thirty. And fifteen. They were going faster and faster.

There was no time to think. There was nothing to do except gulp fresh air and hope for a miracle.

Something grabbed his ankle.

A hand.

Tim twisted around in the water and saw Pelottinho's face.

Pelottinho was holding Tim's ankle. There weren't two of them going over the waterfall – there were three. They were all going to plunge to their deaths together.

It doesn't matter, thought Tim. He couldn't fight. There was no way to shake off Pelottinho.

Ten feet. Five. Four, three, two. White foam bubbled over their heads. Tim took a deep gulp of breath. He crashed into a rock, rolled over and dropped over the waterfall's lip.

Pelottinho dropped with him.

They fell through the air.

And stopped.

All along the length of the waterfall, bits and pieces had got stuck. They had come rushing down the river from the jungle, tipped over the edge and jammed against the rocks. Sticks and twigs. Bushy leaves. Vivid flowers. A dead anaconda. A bird's nest which had fallen into the river from a tree. A beer bottle which had rolled off a boat. A flip-flop. Most of them stayed stuck for a few seconds, or maybe a minute or two, and then were swept down by the immense power of the water, falling a hundred feet, disappearing into the frothing mass of foam and spray.

But others stayed stuck. Like this branch. Having fallen from a tree into the river, it had been swept downstream. When the branch tipped over the waterfall's lip, it had jammed here, stuck between two protruding rocks.

And in turn, Tim had jammed against the branch, trapped by his arms. He clung desperately to the wood with his right arm and held Grk with his left, gripping Grk's slippery tail between his fingers.

Pelottinho hung from Tim's ankle.

The water crashed over them, roaring and spitting. Like a power shower with a million gallons spilling through the nozzle every second.

The branch groaned and creaked and started to bend.

It couldn't hold their weight. In a moment, the wood would snap. Then all three of them would plunge a hundred feet to their deaths.

Tim looked down and stared into Pelottinho's eyes. Glaring back at him, he could see an expression of

176

passionate hatred. He understood exactly what that expression meant. Pelottinho knew that he had no chance of survival. A few seconds from now, he was going to drop a hundred feet. The waters were waiting to swallow him up. Pelottinho knew that he was about to die – but Pelottinho was determined not to die alone.

I am going to die, said the expression in Pelottinho's eyes, and you are going to die with me.

If Pelottinho had possessed two arms, he could have swung round his other hand to get a better grip. Or he could have reached for the knife gripped between his teeth. But Pelottinho possessed only one hand and it was clamped around Tim's ankle. He couldn't move. He couldn't help himself. All he could do was hang there, pulling Tim downwards, killing them both.

The branch strained. The wood splintered.

Tim could feel his body screaming in agony. He couldn't hold on much longer. In a few seconds, he would have to let go. And then he would plunge down into the boiling morass of water, a hundred feet below. His bones would snap like little twigs and his lungs would fill with water and he would sink under the surface and smack against a rock. A few days or weeks from now, his body would be washed ashore, some miles downstream, limp and sodden.

It wasn't Tim's idea.

He didn't even know what was happening.

All his attention was focused on holding Grk's tail with his left hand and the branch with his right hand.

177

He saw Grk opening his mouth. He saw Grk's small sharp white teeth. They glistened in the sunlight. And he saw Grk's mouth snap shut as Grk buried his teeth in Pelottinho's hand.

Pelottinho's eyes widened. The pain was excruciating.

Grk's jaws clamped together. Tighter and tighter. Piercing the skin. Ripping the nerves.

Pelottinho yelled in agony. Blood popped through his wounds. He couldn't resist. The pain was too much. There was nothing that Pelottinho could do except open his fingers and let go of Tim's ankle. Immediately, gravity and the force of the water swept him away. In an instant, he had fallen a hundred feet, twisting and turning through the air, and plunged into the swirling spray, and vanished in the frothing foam.

Tim saw a final glimpse of his black hair and his one arm, held defiantly upwards, reaching for the sky. And then Pelottinho was gone, swallowed by the bubbling cauldron of the Machado Falls.

Tim could feel the strength fading in his arms.

He couldn't hold on for much longer.

His left arm would lose its strength and he would let go of Grk, who would fall a hundred feet into the boiling water.

Then his right arm would lose its strength and he would fall too.

His muscles ached. Nothing had ever hurt so much.

Tim gritted his teeth. His arms felt as if they were

being twisted and tugged and pulled and grabbed.

Tim looked at Grk.

Grk stared back.

Something in Grk's black eyes gave Tim strength. He didn't know what it was. He didn't know why. But he felt stronger.

He pulled with all his might.

He could feel his muscles ripping like paper.

Holding the branch with his right hand, he pulled Grk with his left hand, lifting him up to the level of his shoulders. Grk knew exactly what to do: he chomped a piece of Tim's T-shirt between his teeth and clung on.

Now Tim had two arms free.

He swung his left arm up and grabbed the branch. Using both hands, he pulled himself up. Grk dangled from his chest. Water spilled over them. Tim was soaked through. His hands were slippery. But he managed to haul himself up to the branch, swing his legs over and sit astride the tree like a rider on a horse.

Tim leaned back. Grk squatted on his lap. On either side, water crashed down. Tim realised that he couldn't do anything more to help himself. He couldn't go up and he couldn't go down. He could hardly even think: the water was so loud that it had deafened him and drowned out every thought in his head. But he was alive. They were alive. Nothing else mattered.

Chapter 35

Seven hours later, a man dangled down the face of the waterfall on a long rope. He was wearing a crash helmet and an orange plastic waterproof suit. A taut rope was wrapped around his middle. The other end of the rope was fifty feet above him, tied to a pulley inside a police rescue helicopter.

The policeman wrapped a harness round Tim, another round Grk, and clipped both of them to his own harness. He spoke into his mouthpiece. The rope tautened. The three of them lifted into the air. They swung back and forwards, then soared above the falls.

The helicopter flew across the river, carrying Tim, Grk and the policeman on the end of the rope.

When they reached the bank, the helicopter lowered them to the ground. The policeman unclipped the harness. Tim collapsed on the ground. Grk took a couple of paces, stuck out his tongue and licked Tim's face. Then he collapsed too.

Shane had found a radio in the Pelottis' lorry and summoned the Brazilian police. Shane himself hadn't waited for them to arrive: he had taken the Land Rover and disappeared into the jungle. By now, he must have been two hundred miles away. Before leaving, he had scrawled a quick note on a scrap of paper.

Dear Tim,
Sorry I couldn't stick around but I have a plane to catch. Maybe see you again one day. Give me a call if you're ever down under.
Best wishes
Shane

Later, more police arrived in several speedboats. They boarded the cruiser. In the cabins, they found forty sacks, stuffed with banknotes. The money was wet but otherwise undamaged.

They also found José and Pablo Pelotti. José had concussion and Pablo had a broken leg. Both surrendered without a struggle.

Pelottinho's body was never found.

According to the police, no one could possibly have survived that long plunge into the heart of the waterfall. If his bones hadn't been smashed into a thousand fragments, he would have drowned in the raging waters.

The police scrawled a note on his file:

'Felipe Pelotti, also known as Pelottinho, disappeared at the Machado Falls, presumed dead.'

Chapter 36

The helicopter delivered Tim, Grk and Zito to the nearest airport. From there, they were flown to Rio. At the airport, a crowd of police, journalists and onlookers awaited them.

Mr and Mrs Malt wrapped their arms around Tim.

Grk wagged his tail and rolled on the floor, waiting for Natascha to tickle his belly.

Max shook hands with Zito and practised a few of the Portuguese words that he had learnt over the past couple of days. '*Bom dia*,' he said. '*Meu nome é Max.*' Which means 'Good morning, my name is Max.'

'Me Zito,' replied Zito in English. 'Nice meet you.'

When Tim had been hugged by Mr Malt and Mrs Malt, and after he had promised that he would never, ever, run away from his family again, he turned to Max and Natascha. He said, 'Hi there.'

'Hi, Tim,' said Max. 'Good to see you.'

Natascha didn't say anything. She just had a huge grin on her face.

'I have to say one thing to you two,' said Tim. 'I'm really sorry.'

'Sorry?' said Max.

'For what?' said Natascha.

'For going after the Pelottis without you.'

Max burst out laughing. Natascha shook her head and

said, 'Don't be ridiculous, Tim. We're so happy.'

'Really?'

'Really,' said Natascha. 'It doesn't matter who caught them. All that matters is they've been caught.'

Before they could talk any more, Chief Careca clapped his hands, calling for silence. When everyone was quiet, he unrolled a sheet of paper and started reading. 'On behalf of the Brazilian government,' said Chief Careca, 'I have been authorised to thank you for all your valiant efforts. You have saved us from three of the most vicious, brutal and ruthless criminals ever to set foot on this continent. You have rescued the banks of Brazil. You have saved the good name of the Brazilian police force. From the bottom of our hearts, we thank you.'

'That's okay,' said Tim in a low voice. Everyone was staring at him. It was quite embarrassing.

'As you know,' continued Chief Careca, 'the Brazilian government offered a reward for the capture of the Pelotti brothers. Dead or alive. With great pleasure, I should like to present you with this cheque.' Chief Careca reached into his top pocket and pulled out a white envelope. 'Spend it wisely.' With a smile, Chief Careca handed the envelope to Tim.

'Thank you very much,' said Tim. He opened the envelope and looked at the cheque. When he saw the amount of money written on the cheque, his eyes widened. 'Wow,' he said. 'This is fantastic. That's a lot of money.'

'You deserve it,' said Chief Careca. 'You are a young man of exceptional courage and intelligence.'

'Thanks,' said Tim. 'Thanks a lot. There's just one problem. You put the wrong name on it.'

'The wrong name?'

Tim nodded. He handed the cheque to Chief Careca.

Chief Careca opened the envelope and stared at the cheque. 'But it says on the cheque, Timothy Malt.'

'Exactly,' said Tim.

Chief Careca was confused. 'Your name is not Timothy Malt?'

Tim nodded. 'My name is Timothy Malt.'

Chief Careca was even more confused. 'Excuse me, but I don't understand.'

'The name on the cheque should be his,' said Tim, and pointed at Zito.

When Zito realised what was happening, he clapped his hands and chortled with laughter. Then he ran to Tim and wrapped his arms around him. 'Thank you, Tim. Thank you.'

'It's all right,' said Tim. 'You need the money more than me.'

After a whispered consultation with several of his junior officers, Chief Careca agreed to change the name on the cheque. The money would be given to Zito.

'Brazil owes you a huge debt,' said Chief Careca to Tim. 'Even if you don't want the reward, we still wish to repay you. So, what will you have? Perhaps you want a private beach?'

'No, thanks,' said Tim.

'Or a piece of the rain forest?'

'Not really,' said Tim.

184

'Do you want to stay for another month in the Copacabana Castle?'

'I'd rather go home,' said Tim.

'You don't want to stay in Brazil any more? You don't like Brazil?'

'Of course I like Brazil,' said Tim. 'I love Brazil. But I want to sleep in my own bed. I want to play on my computer. I want to walk round the block with Grk. I just want to do normal things.'

That night, the Malts, the Raffifis and Grk stayed in the Copacabana Castle. Zito and Júnior joined them for supper in the restaurant.

Zito and Júnior had already tasted every dish on the menu, so they advised the others what to eat. Of course, neither Zito nor Júnior had ever actually eaten in the restaurant; they had only picked the scraps from the hotel's dustbins.

Together, everyone discussed the arrangements that Zito had made with an estate agent. The following morning, Zito was going to tour apartments. Júnior was going to live with him. They would rent a big place with a view of the ocean. 'Come and stay whenever you want,' said Zito. 'You will be my guests.'

At the end of the meal, all seven of them slumped back in their chairs, their bellies so full that they could hardly breathe.

'That was delicious,' said Natascha.

'I would have preferred a good honest Stanislavian dumpling,' said Max. 'But this comes a close second.'

185

Tim turned to Zito and asked, 'Does it feel good to be sitting here? Is it better than eating out of the dustbins?'

Zito thought for a moment. Then he shrugged his shoulders. 'I like this,' he said, gesturing at the white tablecloths and the silver cutlery. 'And I like that,' he said, gesturing at the candles and the waiters. 'But the food . . . ' Zito shrugged his shoulders. 'You know what? The food taste the same on the plate or in the dustbin.'

Chapter 37

It was a typical English afternoon. The sky was grey and a few plump drops of rain tapped against the windows.

Mr and Mrs Malt were staying late in their offices. Natascha was upstairs in her bedroom, hunched over her diary, writing quickly, describing the events of the past few days. Max was in the garden, knocking a tennis ball against the back wall. Tim was slumped on the sofa in the sitting room and Grk was lying on the floor.

Grk licked his paws. Tim leaned forward and stared at the TV screen. A zombie stared back.

The zombie opened his mouth and whispered, 'Are you ready to die?'

'Not right now,' said Tim. He pressed a button on his remote control. A small grenade fizzed across the screen. The zombie exploded.

Tim grinned. It was good to be back home. He pressed another button and headed down the dark tunnels, searching for more zombies.